Jessica was lying on her bed, listening to the sounds of her parents and Elizabeth talking downstairs. Although they were just in another part of the house, it felt to Jessica as though they were in another part of the world.

At least Adam Marvel understood. Adam was on Jessica's side. Adam cared about *her*. He had told her that she was outgrowing her friends and her family, just the way a snail outgrows its shell. And like the snail, she would have to find a new shell—one that was empty and waiting for her.

Jessica rolled on her side. She knew that the new shell Adam was talking about was the Good Friends. They needed her. They were waiting for her.

Bantam Books in the Sweet Valley High series
Ask your bookseller for the books you have missed

#1 DOUBLE LOVE
#2 SECRETS
#3 PLAYING WITH FIRE
#4 POWER PLAY
#5 ALL NIGHT LONG
#6 DANGEROUS LOVE
#7 DEAR SISTER
#8 HEARTBREAKER
#9 RACING HEARTS
#10 WRONG KIND OF GIRL
#11 TOO GOOD TO BE TRUE
#12 WHEN LOVE DIES
#13 KIDNAPPED!
#14 DECEPTIONS
#15 PROMISES
#16 RAGS TO RICHES
#17 LOVE LETTERS
#18 HEAD OVER HEELS
#19 SHOWDOWN
#20 CRASH LANDING!
#21 RUNAWAY
#22 TOO MUCH IN LOVE
#23 SAY GOODBYE
#24 MEMORIES
#25 NOWHERE TO RUN
#26 HOSTAGE!
#27 LOVESTRUCK
#28 ALONE IN THE CROWD
#29 BITTER RIVALS
#30 JEALOUS LIES
#31 TAKING SIDES
#32 THE NEW JESSICA
#33 STARTING OVER
#34 FORBIDDEN LOVE
#35 OUT OF CONTROL
#36 LAST CHANCE
#37 RUMORS
#38 LEAVING HOME
#39 SECRET ADMIRER
#40 ON THE EDGE
#41 OUTCAST
#42 CAUGHT IN THE MIDDLE

#43 HARD CHOICES
#44 PRETENSES
#45 FAMILY SECRETS
#46 DECISIONS
#47 TROUBLEMAKER
#48 SLAM BOOK FEVER
#49 PLAYING FOR KEEPS
#50 OUT OF REACH
#51 AGAINST THE ODDS
#52 WHITE LIES
#53 SECOND CHANCE
#54 TWO-BOY WEEKEND
#55 PERFECT SHOT
#56 LOST AT SEA
#57 TEACHER CRUSH
#58 BROKENHEARTED
#59 IN LOVE AGAIN
#60 THAT FATAL NIGHT
#61 BOY TROUBLE
#62 WHO'S WHO?
#63 THE NEW ELIZABETH
#64 THE GHOST OF
     TRICIA MARTIN
#65 TROUBLE AT HOME
#66 WHO'S TO BLAME?
#67 THE PARENT PLOT
#68 THE LOVE BET
#69 FRIEND AGAINST FRIEND
#70 MS. QUARTERBACK
#71 STARRING JESSICA!
#72 ROCK STAR'S GIRL
#73 REGINA'S LEGACY
#74 THE PERFECT GIRL
#75 AMY'S TRUE LOVE
#76 MISS TEEN SWEET VALLEY
#77 CHEATING TO WIN
#78 THE DATING GAME
#79 THE LONG-LOST BROTHER
#80 THE GIRL THEY BOTH LOVED
#81 ROSA'S LIE
#82 KIDNAPPED BY THE CULT!

Super Editions: PERFECT SUMMER
                SPECIAL CHRISTMAS
                SPRING BREAK
                MALIBU SUMMER
                WINTER CARNIVAL
                SPRING FEVER

Super Thrillers: DOUBLE JEOPARDY
                 ON THE RUN
                 NO PLACE TO HIDE
                 DEADLY SUMMER

Super Stars: LILA'S STORY
                BRUCE'S STORY
                ENID'S STORY
                OLIVIA'S STORY

Magna Edition: THE WAKEFIELDS OF SWEET VALLEY

SWEET VALLEY High®

KIDNAPPED BY THE CULT!

Written by
Kate William

Created by
FRANCINE PASCAL

BANTAM BOOKS
NEW YORK • TORONTO • LONDON • SYDNEY • AUCKLAND

RL 6, age 12 and up

KIDNAPPED BY THE CULT!
A Bantam Book / February 1992

Produced by Daniel Weiss Associates, Inc.
33 West 17th Street
New York, NY 10011

Cover art by James Mathewuse

ISBN 0-553-29228-5

Published simultaneously in the United States and Canada

Bantam Books are published by Bantam Books, a division of Bantam
Doubleday Dell Publishing Group, Inc. Its trademark, consisting of the
words "Bantam Books" and the portrayal of a rooster, is Registered
in U.S. Patent and Trademark Office and in other countries. Marca
Registrada. Bantam Books, 666 Fifth Avenue, New York, New York
10103.

PRINTED IN THE UNITED STATES OF AMERICA

OPM   0 9 8 7 6 5 4 3 2 1

To the Children of Rosie and Harry's Place

One

"It was a fantastic party!" Cara Walker said to Lila Fowler. "Those Christmas lights you strung across the living room were *so* romantic."

Lila Fowler smiled. "What can I say? I'm a great hostess." Lila was the daughter of one of the richest men in Sweet Valley, and modesty was not part of her personality.

Amy Sutton shook her head. "The barbecue was even better," she said. "Especially when Winston and Ken jumped into the pool with all their clothes on!"

"Friday night was terrific, too," Sandra Bacon said. She rolled her eyes. "Whose idea was it to order that chocolate chip pizza?" She turned to Lila. "It's a good thing your dad wasn't there!"

Lila's father had left on Friday afternoon for a week-long business trip, and Lila had decided to make the most of his absence. Friday night she

1

had invited her favorite Pi Beta Alpha sisters to a sleepover, Saturday night she threw a huge party, and on Sunday she invited several friends for a barbecue and pool party.

Now it was Monday morning, and Jessica Wakefield stood in the hallway of Sweet Valley High with Lila, Cara, Amy, and Sandra and listened miserably as they talked about the fantastic weekend. Jessica hadn't been to any of the weekend's parties because her parents had grounded her for three weeks, and she still had almost one week to go.

"Well, it sounds like you all had a good weekend," she said flatly.

"Good?" Lila said, laughing. "It was amazing."

"It was the best weekend I've had in a long time," Amy agreed.

Jessica tossed her shoulder-length golden blond hair. "I'm glad you didn't let the fact that I was locked in my room with a math book stop you from enjoying yourselves," she said, sulking.

"It was too bad you couldn't be there," Sandra said sympathetically.

Cara nodded. "Especially since you had to miss the Pi Beta dance, too."

Jessica scowled. Her parents, ignoring the fact that she was president of the sorority, had grounded her starting the day of the Pi Beta Alpha induction ceremony and dance.

Lila shrugged. "It's your own fault, Jessica," she said. "You really have no one else to blame."

Jessica's scowl deepened. It just so happened

2

that she could think of several other people to blame.

First of all, she could blame her parents. They were being completely unreasonable. What had she done that was so awful? Sure, she had failed a couple of math tests. So what? Everyone—except Jessica's twin, Elizabeth—failed a test now and then.

Which brought Jessica to the second person she could blame: Elizabeth Wakefield. Jessica and her twin might look identical, from their sparkling blue-green eyes and silky blond hair, but in reality they were as different as night and day. Elizabeth was mature and responsible. She was a straight-A student and a reporter for *The Oracle*, Sweet Valley High's newspaper. Jessica loved to have fun, and lately, it seemed, got into nothing but trouble. As far as Jessica could tell, her parents thought Elizabeth was perfect and that Jessica couldn't do anything right. Jessica was sure that if her identical twin weren't so perfect, her parents would be less critical of her.

Jessica frowned as she looked at her friends. Thirdly, she could blame them. What sort of friends were they, anyway? They knew she was grounded; did they have to cram every major social event they could think of into the few weeks when Jessica couldn't go? Would real friends act like that? No, Jessica told herself. Real friends would have stuck by her. Real friends would have spent their free time cheering her up. After all, these were the girls who had encouraged her to go shopping when she should have been studying, the girls who always insisted she go to the beach with them instead of doing her homework. How insensitive, spoiled, and self-centered could you get?

"Some friends," Jessica muttered, and marched away.

By lunchtime that day, however, Jessica's mood had changed again. She had decided that she probably shouldn't be angry with her friends. After all, it might not have been Jessica's fault that her parents had grounded her, but it wasn't really her friends' fault, either. And she did still have five more days before her parents would let her out of the house for anything other than school or cheerleading practice. That meant five long, boring evenings in the split-level prison on Calico Drive. Five evenings spent all by herself with a textbook while her friends were having a great time hanging out at Lila's. Just the thought of it made Jessica feel like crying. It might as well have been five years. Being grounded didn't get easier; it got harder. She would love to go for a pizza with the cheerleaders! She would die to go to a movie with her boyfriend, Sam Woodruff! She would even consider visiting a museum with Elizabeth, just to get out of the house.

Jessica realized that she would never make it through those last five days. Not unless she could convince her friends to call her and visit her. Maybe if she was really nice to them, she could even convince them not to do anything really wonderful until Saturday, when Jessica would finally be free.

Jessica arrived at the cafeteria with a bounce in her step and a smile and went over to the table where Lila, Amy, and Cara were sitting.

"Hi there!" Jessica said cheerfully, sounding like her usual self. She slid into the empty seat beside Lila. "What's happening?"

"We were just deciding what to do this week, before my father comes home," Lila said.

Jessica's smile remained steady.

Cara nodded. "Only we can't decide when to have another sleepover."

Jessica's smile faded just a little.

"Because of the pool party Friday night," Amy explained. "We can't fit everything in." She looked straight at Jessica. "Not and keep up our schoolwork, too," she added.

Jessica unwrapped her sandwich without looking up. "So skip the pool party," she said. "You can always have another one."

"If it isn't soon, though, I won't be able to come," Cara said quickly. Something in her voice made her friends all turn to her expectantly. Cara blushed. "I was going to wait to tell you this," she said, "but I guess now is as good a time as any. My mother just told me last night that she and I will be going to London." Cara looked around, smiling.

There were a few seconds of stunned silence.

"London?" Jessica repeated. "London, England?"

Cara nodded. "We'll be there for a week."

5

Jessica couldn't believe this. Wasn't it bad enough that Lila was having another sleepover *and* a pool party? Now Cara Walker was going to London!

"Oh, you're *so* lucky, Cara," Lila gushed. "London is great, believe me. There's so much to do! You'll have a wonderful time," she assured her.

"I'm so jealous!" Amy squealed. "I've always dreamed of going to London. English boys have the cutest accents. Don't you think so, Jess?"

"Umph," Jessica said from behind her sandwich. Even though it tasted as if it had turned to sand, Jessica was grateful she had a mouthful of food. At least it meant she didn't have to speak. If she had to speak, she wouldn't be able to hide her disappointment. Why had she been born to parents who thought going out to dinner was a big deal, while Cara had a mother who just suddenly decided to go to London? Life was unfair. Here she was, born to travel, and she couldn't even leave the house! Jessica dropped her unfinished sandwich onto the table.

"Cheer up, Jess," said Cara. "You're only grounded for a few more days."

"Five," Jessica hissed, pushing her tray away.

"Five," Cara corrected herself. "Well, that's not so long."

Lila reached into her bag and took out a notebook and a pen. "We'll have to make a list of all the things we have to do to get you ready for London," she said to Cara.

Amy beat on the table with her fingertips. "This

is so exciting." She laughed. "I almost feel like I'm going, too."

Jessica got to her feet. No one looked up. Lila was telling Cara where the best dress shops were in London, and Amy was trying to talk with an English accent.

"Well," Jessica said, "I've got to go to the library."

Lila and Cara nodded without even glancing in her direction.

"Or maybe I'll go throw myself in front of a truck," she said.

When she had first been grounded, Jessica had looked forward to Tuesday afternoons. Tuesday afternoon Jessica was allowed to go to cheerleading practice, the only extracurricular activity Mr. and Mrs. Wakefield were letting her continue. Jessica had taken this as a sign of humanity and compassion on her parents' part. They didn't want her to be completely left out, she had told herself. Since then, however, she'd changed her mind.

Her parents must have known that going to practice would only make her feel *more* left out. When the cheerleaders weren't going through their routines, they were making plans for after practice or later in the evening. They went on and on about all the things they were doing that weekend. It was torture.

And that Tuesday was the worst.

While they were changing into their uniforms, Amy and Cara kept talking about the sleepover

Lila was having the following night. Lila was going to show the pictures she had taken the last time she was in London, and Lila's cook was going to make fish and chips in honor of Cara.

Lila turned to Jessica. "I really wish you could come, too," she said. "Especially since you may never get to London yourself."

Jessica banged her locker shut so quickly, she nearly caught Lila's hair in it.

All during practice, Jessica fumed. She shouldn't have come, she decided. Cheerleading was boring. The routines were boring. The other cheerleaders were boring. She should have gone straight home.

"Jessica!" called Robin Wilson, who was co-captain with Jessica. "Pay attention, will you? You're mixing up the cheers."

Jessica glowered. She had written half the cheers herself, and now Robin was accusing her of getting them wrong!

Maria Santelli leaned over Jessica's shoulder. "Loosen up, Jess! You've got as much spring as a brick wall."

A ripple of laughter moved along the two rows of cheerleaders. Jessica's cheeks burned and she threw her pompoms on the ground in frustration. *I can't do anything right anymore*, she thought as she stormed away.

At least one good thing is happening today, Jessica told herself as she quickly dressed before the other cheerleaders came into the locker room. *At least I'm going to see Sam.*

Sam was picking her up after practice and driving her home. Even before she had been grounded, the fact that Sam went to Bridgewater High and spent so much time on his dirt bike meant that he didn't pay as much attention to Jessica as she would have liked. She had hoped that since she was grounded and couldn't stand in the mud every weekend watching him race, he would come to the house more often. But so far, things hadn't worked out that way.

Jessica waited in the parking lot a good ten minutes before Sam finally drove up. "I was just beginning to think you'd forgotten me," she said with a laugh as she slid in beside him.

Jessica waited for him to say something like *I could never forget you, Jess.* "I'm sorry I'm late, Jess, but I'm having some trouble with my bike," he said instead.

"Your bike?" she asked.

Sam nodded. "Remember I told you I took a spill on Sunday?"

"Uh-huh," Jessica said. In fact, she didn't remember. Her parents thought she spent more time on the telephone than she did studying, and so they had limited her to incoming calls no longer than ten minutes. She had to pack a lot into those ten minutes, and mostly it wasn't listening.

Sam made a face. "Well, it looks like the damage is worse than I thought."

"Which means what?" Jessica asked, eyeing him suspiciously.

9

"Which means I have to get home soon so I can work on it tonight."

"Tonight?" Jessica couldn't keep the shrillness out of her voice. "But I thought you were coming to my house for dinner."

Sam reached for her hand as they stopped at a light, but she pulled it away. "I'm sorry, Jess, I really am. But you know I've got a big race on Saturday. I've got to get the bike fixed in time."

"You can fix it any other night this week," Jessica protested. "I thought you were going to spend some time with me for a change. I haven't seen you for days!"

"I'm really sorry, Jess," Sam said. "You know I've missed you. But this is really important."

"More important than I am?" Jessica asked. There was a tone in her voice and a look in her eyes that her family would instantly have recognized as dangerous.

Sam laughed. "How could I compare a dirt bike to one of the two most beautiful girls in southern California?" He leaned over and kissed her cheek. "The one who goes out with me."

"You mean the one who doesn't go out anywhere," Jessica grumbled.

When Jessica went to the school parking lot to meet her sister on Wednesday afternoon, she found Todd Wilkins sitting in the passenger seat of the Fiat the twins shared, talking excitedly with Elizabeth.

Elizabeth opened the door so Jessica could

10

squeeze into the cramped space in the back. "Todd's coming home with us today," Elizabeth announced breezily.

"Oh," said Jessica. The last thing she needed was to watch Todd and Elizabeth being the perfect couple. They could be pretty sickening at the best of times, but especially when her own romance wasn't doing too well. She hadn't spoken to Sam since he had dropped her off the day before.

Elizabeth turned to her twin with a smile. "There's a new bowling team starting up at school, and Todd and I have decided to join!" She seemed inexplicably happy about this. "You know, bowling shirts, those awesome shoes, lots of greasy food at the bowling alley," Elizabeth continued, laughing.

As far as Jessica was concerned, bowling was a sweaty sport, with absolutely no fashion potential. "I'm surprised you have the time for another activity," she said.

"Not only will we get to improve our games, we'll be able to spend more time together, too," Todd said, grinning.

"Well, isn't that just wonderful," Jessica said, staring out the window.

"I hear the coach is excellent but very demanding," Todd was saying as Elizabeth pulled into the Wakefields' driveway. "Just think of all the hours of practice we'll have to put in!" he added with a mischievous grin as Jessica clambered out of the car.

Jessica stormed into the house, up the stairs,

and into her room. But she couldn't escape them. Barricaded in her room, she could still hear them downstairs, talking and laughing. How did they find so much to talk about? After all the time Elizabeth and Todd had been dating, she would have thought they'd be sick of talking to each other by then. With a heavy sigh, she got up and went out to the hallway. "Do you two think you could be a little quieter down there?" she called. "Some of us are trying to do our homework."

"Sure, Jess. Sorry about that," Todd called back.

Jessica stomped back into her room. At least Todd would be going home soon, she told herself. That was some consolation.

But Todd, Jessica discovered when she went down to supper, was *not* going home soon. Mrs. Wakefield, probably to punish Jessica even more than she already had, had asked Todd to join them.

"I don't believe this," Jessica muttered as she slammed the plates down on the table. "Aren't you afraid Elizabeth's going to fall behind in her schoolwork if she spends so much time with Todd?"

Mrs. Wakefield passed her the silverware. "I think we can risk one evening," she said evenly. "Elizabeth isn't failing math."

Jessica threw the knives and forks into place. Elizabeth, Elizabeth, Elizabeth. Elizabeth with her straight A's. Elizabeth with her award-winning work on *The Oracle*. Elizabeth with her perfect boyfriend. And where was Jessica's perfect boyfriend? Probably lying on the floor of his garage with his head under a motorcycle. Jessica bounced the salt and pepper shakers into place.

"Maybe you and Sam would like to come bowling with us sometime," Elizabeth suggested after they had all sat down to eat.

Jessica stared at her blankly. *"Bowling?"* she asked, as though Elizabeth had suggested cobra wrestling.

But before Jessica could explain to her sister exactly what she thought of bowling, Mr. Wakefield broke into the conversation. "I think maybe Jessica has enough to do getting her grades up at the moment," he said, with a significant look in her direction.

Jessica stared back at him in horror. He might as well have picked up his chicken leg and slapped her in the face with it. Wasn't it bad enough that everyone was always on her back about something? Now her father had to embarrass her in front of Todd, too.

"I wouldn't be caught dead bowling!" Jessica shouted as she pushed back her chair and rushed out of the room.

Two

The end of the week went no better for Jessica than the beginning. On Thursday she picked a fight with Elizabeth at breakfast, argued with Lila and Amy at lunch, and ended the day by hanging up on Sam. Friday she moped.

But on Saturday Jessica woke up feeling happy and excited. She had grown so accustomed to being miserable that for a few minutes she couldn't remember why she felt so good. She lay in bed, staring out the window at the gray and drizzly morning. Was it Christmas? Was it her birthday? Was she buying a new outfit today? Was there a big party tonight? And then it came to her: today she was a free woman again!

Jessica jumped out of bed. "Look out, world!" she cried. "I'm back!"

It didn't matter that it was raining; this was the brightest day of the year. She had worked it all out in her mind. With the exception of the two hours it would take her to get dressed, and the ten minutes she knew she'd better put into doing her weekend chores, Jessica was going to spend every waking minute of the day with Sam.

They were meeting at the Dairi Burger for breakfast. Jessica figured their breakfast would be long and leisurely, with a lot of looking into each other's eyes. After that, she had decided, they would spend the rest of the morning shopping. There was a café beside the artificial waterfall at the mall that always made Jessica think of Paris. They would have lunch there. Then, if the rain had stopped, they might get in a game of tennis. If not, they would catch an afternoon movie—a love story, of course. Jessica was certain that by evening the weather would have cleared. She and Sam would have supper by candlelight at one of those romantic restaurants along the coast. Afterwards they would stroll along the moonlit beach. Just thinking of it made her sigh out loud. They would hold hands. She would lean her head on Sam's shoulder and he would tell her how much he had missed her. They would draw a heart in the sand and write their initials in it.

Jessica sang in the shower. She hummed while she decided what she would wear. Turquoise to match her eyes? Pink and white to show off her tan? Or bright yellow to match her mood? She twirled in front of the full-length mirror. Green, she finally decided. Green made her hair look even blonder. And green was Sam's favorite color.

Elizabeth came into the bathroom while Jessica was putting the finishing touches on her makeup.

Jessica greeted her with an enormous smile. "Good morning, Liz!" she said. Looking at Jessica, no one would ever guess she had spent the past three weeks skulking around the house like a ghost.

Elizabeth stared at her twin. "Well," she said, "it's nice to see you smiling for a change."

Jessica looked surprised. "Me?" she asked innocently. "Of course I'm smiling. Why shouldn't I be?"

"Oh, no reason," Elizabeth said, grinning. "It's just that I thought you said you would never smile again."

Jessica turned to her sister. "And everyone says *I'm* the one with the wild imagination."

"I can't believe it!" Jessica shrieked as she threw herself into the booth next to Sam. "I'm out of the house and there isn't a schoolbook in sight!"

"That's right," he said. "Just donuts and coffee."

Jessica peered around him to catch her reflection in the wall mirror. "Do you think I look pale after having been put away for so long?"

Sam grinned. "I think you look wonderful!" he said sincerely. "And not only does seeing you make me the happiest guy in the world, I know you're going to bring me luck today."

"Luck?" Jessica asked. "You don't need luck to go shopping," she teased. "You just need money."

"Shopping?" Sam asked. "What does shopping have to do with anything?"

"I haven't been to the mall in over three weeks," she said. "What else would we do this morning?"

"Jessica," he said slowly. "Don't tell me you forgot."

"Forgot what?" she asked with an impish grin. "You don't think I've forgotten how to shop, do you?"

"Jessica," Sam said, "I'm not talking about shopping. I'm talking about the race."

"Race?" she repeated. "What race?"

"*The* race," explained Sam. "The race I've been getting ready for all week."

Get a grip on yourself, Jessica, she told herself. *There must be some sort of misunderstanding. You've been locked in the house for so long that you're delirious.*

"What?" she asked, trying to control the squeak in her voice. "Are you saying that you're racing? *Today?*"

"Jess," Sam said patiently, "you knew there was a big meet today. I've been talking about it for days. That's why I was so worried about getting my bike fixed in time."

She should have known better than to wake up smiling. She should have known something would happen to ruin everything. She and Sam hadn't been out together for ages, and he wanted to spend the day on his dumb bike!

"But what about me?" she screeched. "I've been chained in my room for days and days.

17

What am I supposed to do while you're at your stupid meet?"

Sam blinked in surprise. "Well, I thought you'd come along. You know," he added lamely, "cheer me on."

"But it's raining," Jessica grumbled. "Do you expect me to stand in the rain for hours, all by myself, on my first day of freedom, catching pneumonia while you have a good time?"

"But I thought you liked coming to races," Sam protested. "You always said—"

Jessica cut him off. "What I'd like," she announced as she edged out of the booth, "is to spend a little time with you for a change. I thought today was going to be *our* day. Not yours and your bike's." She snatched her purse from the table and marched toward the door.

Sam was right behind her. "Jessica!" he called. "Jessica, wait!"

Don't turn around, Jessica told herself. *Just get out of here as fast as you can.* She banged through the doors of the Dairi Burger and strode across the parking lot.

"Jessica!" Sam yelled. "Wait up!"

Jessica jumped into the Fiat and slammed the door. She didn't look at Sam even though he was pounding on the window. She started the engine and headed for the exit. She knew better than to stop and listen to him. One minute he would be telling her how much he cared about her, and the next minute she would be standing up to her ankles in mud watching him fly by on his bike.

Jessica ground the gears as she accelerated

away from Sam. She was miserably unhappy and she was going to stay that way!

"All right, Sam," she said out loud as the Fiat roared along the street. "If you don't want to go shopping with me, I'll go by myself!"

She took the turnoff to the Valley Mall. Jessica was sure that the spacious walkways and colorful stores would cheer her up.

"You think I have nothing better to do than to hang around watching you, but you're wrong," Jessica continued out loud.

As she talked, Jessica realized it felt good to say all the things she had been keeping bottled up inside.

"And as for you, Amy Sutton and Lila Fowler," she shouted, "I don't think I've ever known two more selfish and spoiled people. All the time I was grounded, did you ever come to see me? Did you ever give one thought to how I was suffering?"

The Fiat came to a stop at an intersection. "No!" Jessica answered herself. "No, you just kept right on having your dumb parties." She banged on the steering wheel and accidentally sounded the horn; the driver in the next car turned to look at her. "And you call yourselves my friends!" she yelled. "Some friends you are! Some sister," she added, suddenly remembering Elizabeth. "Who told Mom and Dad about my math grades?"

The light changed and the lane she was in moved forward. Jessica turned her attention to her parents.

"And I'm totally fed up with being compared

19

to Elizabeth all the time," Jessica said. "You may think she's absolutely perfect, but the truth is that she's *dull*! She thinks that rearranging her closet is exciting. I'm the one with the flair and the zest for life! I'm the one with the great sense of humor! I'm the one with the terrific sense of color and design! I'm the one everyone thinks is so much fun! So what if I don't get straight A's? Albert Einstein failed math, too, you know. Do you think his parents grounded him for that?"

The car came to a stop. "No one appreciates me!" Jessica yelled. Suddenly, she was aware that someone was staring at her. She looked around in some surprise. Two middle-aged women, their arms full of packages, were watching her as they got into their car. Somehow, she had not only arrived at the mall, she had actually parked the car. Jessica stared back at the women. "What are you looking at?" Jessica muttered under her breath as she slammed the door of the Fiat behind her. "Haven't you ever seen a teenager before?" *How typical*, she thought as she hurried into the mall. *Even strangers disapprove of me.*

Jessica immediately headed toward her favorite shop, Bibi's. She knew that as soon as she saw its bright lights and the expensive clothes displayed in the window, she would feel better.

But instead of leaping with joy at the first sight of Bibi's, Jessica's heart sank with sadness. Standing in front of the boutique, his arm around a pretty blonde, was a boy who reminded her of Sam. At the same time, just emerging from the shop was a group of girls carrying Bibi's shopping bags and laughing happily—just as she and her friends used to do. An enormous lump formed in Jessica's throat. She was right! Everyone was loved and happy except for her. With a strangled sob, Jessica burst into tears.

Jessica Wakefield was not the sort of person who cried in public. If you had to cry, she believed, it was better to do it in the privacy of your own room, where no one could see your red eyes or blotchy skin.

That is, the old, popular, and adored Jessica Wakefield didn't cry in public. But the new, misunderstood, and unloved Jessica did. She was far too upset now to worry about the state of her mascara. Weeping loudly, she flung herself onto the first bench she came to, and collapsed in a flood of tears.

Jessica had no idea how long she had been sitting there, blotting her eyes with tissues, before she realized that there was someone else on the bench. Her tears finally subsiding, she glanced over cautiously. There, right beside her, was a boy about her age with red hair and freckles. He was looking at her with concern.

"Is there something I can do?" the boy asked. His voice was warm and sympathetic. "You seem so upset."

Of course I'm upset, Jessica wanted to shout at him. Instead she reached into her bag for another tissue. "Don't tell me," she sniffled, "you must be the great detective Sherlock Holmes." She was so agitated that she knocked her oversized shoulder bag to the floor. An assortment of cosmetics, brushes, and cassettes tumbled out. Groaning, Jessica started to stuff them back in.

"Sarcasm doesn't solve anything," the boy said gently. He bent down to help her pick up her things. "You don't have to be defensive," he continued as he handed her the package of tissues. "I know exactly what you're going through, believe me."

Jessica blew her nose. "Oh, sure you do," she said sourly. "You don't even know my name."

"I know that you're feeling very alone right now. Probably your family doesn't understand you. They don't appreciate you."

There was something about this boy's voice that was strangely soothing, almost hypnotic. Jessica found herself listening to him in spite of herself.

"Maybe you're involved in a messed-up, one-sided relationship," the boy went on.

Jessica had been quickly stuffing things back into her bag, but now she slowed down so she could listen. She couldn't remember the last time anyone had sounded so concerned about her.

"Your friends have probably let you down," he said softly. "They think only about themselves. . . ."

Slowly, Jessica raised her eyes to his. "That's amazing," she whispered. "You really do know how I'm feeling."

The boy extended his hand. "My name's Ted," he said with a warm smile.

Jessica, still feeling a little stunned, took Ted's

hand and shook it. He had a firm, strong grip. "I—I'm Jessica," she stammered. She smiled shyly. "I don't understand, though. How can you know so much about me when we've never met before?"

"That's easy," he said. "I've been through the exact same things myself."

Jessica's eyes widened. "You have?"

Ted nodded. "My parents treated me like a child. My friends weren't there when I needed them." He shook his head sadly. "I felt like everyone in the world had let me down. I can remember thinking that I was all alone." His brown eyes were filled with kindness. "That nobody cared what happened to me."

"That's just how I feel," Jessica said. Somehow, she had thought that no one but she had ever been through these things.

Jessica began to tell Ted about her problems. How unreasonable her parents were. How self-centered her friends were. How annoying Elizabeth could be. Ted was incredibly easy to talk to. She couldn't remember ever knowing anyone so totally selfless and sympathetic. He really seemed to understand how she felt, unlike everyone else in her life.

Ted nodded wisely as she told him about Sam. "Just when you most needed Sam to be there for you, he let you down," Ted said.

"That's exactly right," Jessica said.

"A similar thing happened to me," Ted said. "The girl I'd been dating dumped me for someone else."

"That's awful," Jessica said, unable to take her eyes from Ted. "But you're all right now. You seem so . . . so . . ."

"So together?"

Jessica nodded.

"That's because I found some real friends," Ted confided. "Friends who like me for me, who will never let me down."

Jessica listened, almost spellbound, while Ted told her about himself. How he had been so unhappy that he'd run away from home. How he had had no one to turn to, and nowhere to go. And then, one day, a miracle had happened. He had met a man named Adam Marvel. Adam had dedicated his life to helping others. "Adam befriended me," Ted explained. "He didn't criticize me or tell me what to do; he just became my friend. And then he invited me to live with a group of people called the Good Friends." Ted smiled. "And from that moment on my life changed for the better."

Jessica came out of her trance at the mention of the word *group*. Somewhere in the back of her mind she could see her sister looking skeptical. "Group?" Jessica asked. "What kind of group?"

"Oh, it's not a real organization or anything like that," Ted explained quickly. "It's just a bunch of friends living together and helping one another out. We're always there for one another," he said. "That's what counts. That's what makes us special."

"Well, that sounds special to me," Jessica agreed. "There aren't many people you can count on."

Ted snapped his fingers. "Hey," he said excitedly. "I've got a great idea! Why don't you come home with me and meet the group? I know they'd cheer you up."

"Oh, I don't know," Jessica said.

Ted laughed good-naturedly. "Hey, I'm not asking you to join or anything. I'm just inviting you to come for supper."

"Just supper?" Jessica asked. She couldn't help feeling a little tingle of satisfaction when she thought how upset everyone would be if she didn't come home for supper. That would show them. "All right," she agreed, a smile lighting up her face. "What time should I be there?"

That Saturday afternoon, the new bowling club was having an organizational meeting at Guido's. Elizabeth, sitting beside Todd, looked around the table at the six other people gathered there. One or two of them were people she knew vaguely from school, but the rest were no more than faces she had passed in the hall.

How could you not have noticed him before? Elizabeth suddenly asked herself, looking right at Justin Silver, the team coach. Justin was one of the best-looking boys she had ever seen. He had slightly longish blond hair, large gray eyes, and strong, clean features. With a flutter of surprise, Elizabeth realized that Justin, sitting across from her at the table, was smiling at her. For one insane moment, she was afraid that he had read her thoughts. But she quickly realized he was just trying to get her attention so that he could start the meeting.

"I'm really glad to see all of you," Justin began after everyone had introduced themselves. "I just hope you're not here only because you like pizza."

Everyone laughed appreciatively.

Justin went on to explain that Sweet Valley High used to have a pretty good bowling team. "At least we could play in the junior league without actually embarrassing ourselves," he said. "The trouble is, we've lost more than half our members in the last year and the team just sort of fell apart. So we've got all these spare bowling shirts lying around, and we need some people to wear them."

Shelley, a dark-haired sophomore, raised her hand. "What if we're not very good?" she wanted to know.

"It depends what you mean by not very good," Justin said, his gray eyes sparkling. "If you mean you sometimes bounce the ball instead of rolling it, that's a minor problem we can easily overcome."

"What if you throw the ball down the alley and it goes backwards instead?" one of the boys asked.

"No problem," Justin said, laughing. "Just try not to hit me." Then he became serious. "With a little work I can help each one of you improve your game, and together we can put together a decent team." He paused, his eyes coming to rest on Elizabeth. "The most important thing, though, is having a good time."

Three

When she passed Fenno Street, a narrow avenue in the least desirable part of Sweet Valley, Jessica began to feel a little uneasy. The closer Jessica got to the address Ted had given her, the more she wondered whether she was making a mistake. Her brother Steven's old girlfriend, Tricia Martin, who had died tragically of leukemia, had lived around here, but except for her Jessica was sure no one she knew had ever set foot in this section of town. The houses were old and rundown; the cars parked in the driveways were dented and unwashed.

Jessica turned down Cedar Street. This was the worst block yet. One house had a dismantled car rusting in the front yard and another had a broken washing machine on the front porch.

She stopped the Fiat in front of number six and checked the piece of paper in her hand a third

27

time. That was what it said: number six, Cedar Street.

Jessica turned off the ignition, but didn't remove her hand from the key. She stared through the window. This really was the worst of the worst. Number six was a large, ramshackle old house with paint peeling off it in large strips. Instead of steps leading up to the porch, there were cinder blocks. Jessica shuddered. It definitely didn't look like the home of any "good friends" of hers. It looked like the home of the Wicked Witch of the West. *How could anyone live in a place like this?* Jessica asked herself. And what was she doing parked outside of it? Jessica groaned out loud. She wished she were back in the cheery kitchen on Calico Drive, having supper with her family. Or, better yet, she wished she were sitting in the Dairi Burger with Sam, listening to his account of the race. Why had she walked out on him like that? Had she completely lost her mind?

"This is ridiculous," she said out loud. "I'm not going to find people who understand me here. I'm going to find people who shop in thrift stores." Looking more closely, she could see an Indian-print bedspread hanging in the front window, where a curtain should be. Jessica's heart sank even further. "They're probably vegetarians," she told herself. "People who eat nothing but tofu." Jessica had once had a disastrous experience selling tofu beauty products door to door. Selling it had been bad enough. She had no intention of eating the stuff.

Jessica started the engine again. She took a deep breath and put the car in gear. She felt better

28

already. She would hurry home, call Sam, and spend the evening the way normal people spent Saturday nights: going to the movies and eating pizza.

But just as Jessica was about to pull away from the curb, the front door of the old house burst open and Ted appeared on the porch.

"Jessica!" he cried, waving frantically. "Jessica! Here we are! This is the place!"

Jessica froze.

Ted ran down the path toward her. He yanked the car door open. "I'm so glad you found us," he said, grinning. "I was just beginning to worry that you'd gotten lost."

No such luck, Jessica said to herself. She smiled at Ted. "I just wasn't sure this was the right house."

"Oh, it's the right house," said Ted happily. "Can't you see the sign up on the porch?"

Jessica squinted at the house. Nailed to a post was a hand-painted sign: The Good Friends.

"I've told everyone about you," he said, gesturing behind him. "They're dying to meet you."

Jessica switched off the engine. She stepped out of the car. "Oh, me, too," she said. "I'm dying to meet them." At least that was true, she comforted herself. Eating tofu with people who dressed in clothes they had bought from rummage sales and didn't even own a curtain was very close to her idea of death.

"Come on," Ted said as he led her through the front door. "I'll give you the grand tour."

At least the inside of the house looked better

than the outside. In fact, Jessica noticed as she followed Ted into the living room, it was actually cheerful. There were a lot of plants in the windows, and the furniture was covered with bright prints and colorful cushions. The walls were full of posters and paintings.

"Oh, what a nice room!" Jessica exclaimed, unable to conceal her surprise.

Ted smiled proudly. "It is nice, isn't it? We do everything we can for ourselves. We make our own clothes, do our own repairs. We don't have money for extras, so everyone in the group is expected to contribute." He gestured to the walls and the hanging baskets at the windows. "You know. To paint, or macramé, or sew. Something like that. It's what we do in our spare time. Adam says it helps us become total people."

Jessica turned her attention to a corner of the room where two girls sat playing guitars together. They both wore faded jeans and old sweaters.

"That's Agnes and China," said Ted, following her gaze. "They're our musicians." He smiled at Jessica. "We make our own entertainment, too. Adam says that creativity is very important." His tone became almost reverential. "Adam doesn't believe in television. He says it destroys conversation."

Jessica nodded. "Oh, I know what he means," she said. She knew what he meant because it was something her parents were always telling her. Personally, Jessica couldn't see how television destroyed conversation. A lot of her friends' conversation was actually *about* television shows.

"Adam says that a creative person is a happy person." Ted said, taking Jessica's elbow and guiding her down the hallway.

"Oh, sure," Jessica said, wondering briefly if Adam would consider shopping a creative activity. "I'm sure he has a point."

"It's more than a point," said Ted quickly. "It's the truth."

"What's this?" Jessica asked, stopping in front of an enormous chart that took up most of the wall outside the kitchen.

"That's our schedule of weekly chores," Ted explained. "Everyone takes turns doing different household tasks. Adam says that we all have to pull our own weight."

Jessica nodded. With his views about chores and television, Adam was beginning to sound a lot like her parents.

Ted opened the door to the kitchen. "Hi, everyone!" he called. "I want you to meet Jessica Wakefield, the girl I met at the mall."

There were five people bustling around the kitchen, preparing the evening meal. As she had suspected, the members of the Good Friends were, in looks at least, a pretty dowdy bunch. The boys mostly wore faded jeans and old plaid shirts. The girls wore clothes that hadn't been fashionable for at least a year. There was only one blonde in the room, and she didn't even have a tan.

Ted introduced them all—Annie, Anita, Doug,

Brooke, and Charles. "Hi," they all said simultaneously, with big smiles.

Jessica barely caught their names because at that moment she realized that there was a delicious smell filling the air. "Chili!" she exclaimed in relief.

Annie, a quietly pretty, brown-haired girl, looked up, blushing slightly. "It's Adam's favorite," she explained. "Chili and cornbread." She glanced at the old clock over the sink. "Only we're beginning to worry that he won't be back in time. He works so hard, he barely gives himself time to eat."

Jessica was starting to relax. Except for the lack of curtains and television, this place seemed pretty normal after all.

"Come on," Ted said, taking her hand. "I want you to meet everyone else before it's time to eat."

In the dining room Mick and David were setting the table. In the study Lilly and Brian were discussing a book. "You two really should join us," Brian said excitedly. "This is the book Adam was telling us about the other night. It's really significant."

Mercifully, Ted kept going. With all the homework she had been doing lately, Jessica had had enough of books to last her a lifetime.

Ted took her upstairs and showed her the bedrooms. Every room contained a desk, a dresser, and several beds. Once again, Indian-print spreads and plants were hung at the windows, and the walls were decorated with pictures and posters. Every room was as neat as Elizabeth's bedroom at home. Not one of them had its own phone.

"What's in there?" Jessica asked as they passed the one door that had remained shut during their tour.

"That's Adam's room," Ted said in hushed tones. "He needs a place where he can work in total peace."

"Oh, of course," Jessica said, following Ted back down the stairs. She imagined that Adam must be around her parents' age. People that old needed peace and quiet.

As they reentered the living room Jessica realized that there was something missing from the Good Friends' house besides a television set and a VCR: noise! There had to be almost twenty people living here, and yet it was practically silent. There were only four people in the Wakefield home most of the time, but compared to this, the noise they made was deafening. And everyone was so polite. Jessica couldn't imagine slamming a door or shouting at anyone in this house the way she did at home.

"It's so quiet!" she whispered to Ted. "Doesn't anybody ever yell or scream here?"

Ted gave her a puzzled smile. "We never argue," he told her simply. "Adam says that people who really love and understand one another don't need to raise their voices."

Jessica remembered all the times people had raised their voices at her in the past few weeks. *See!* she told herself. *I knew no one really loved or understood me!*

*　　*　　*

Dinner was warm and friendly. Jessica sat between Ted and Brian, and across from Annie and a rather sulky-looking girl named Susan. Next to Annie was a thin, intense boy called Sky, and next to him was a plain young woman named Mary.

Not only was everyone exceptionally nice to Jessica, they also seemed to be genuinely interested in her. She was kept busy for most of the meal telling the others all about herself, an activity she always enjoyed.

"So you see," she concluded, looking from one pair of sympathetic, understanding eyes to the next, "everyone's against me. No one really cares about me at all."

Mary smiled shyly. "I don't think I've ever known a cheerleader before."

"Me, either," Sky said. "To tell you the truth, I never thought cheerleaders had problems like other people."

"Then you haven't been listening to Adam very carefully," Brian said sternly but kindly. "Adam says that everyone has problems. What makes us different is the way we handle them."

"That's right," Ted said. "Whether we share our problems—and our joys—with others, or are selfish and keep them to ourselves."

Mary and Adam murmured their agreement. Only Susan said nothing. Every time Jessica looked over at her, she caught her looking back. Next to the friendliness of everyone else, Jessica

34

couldn't help feeling that Susan seemed almost hostile.

"You're right," Sky admitted. "I was doing what Adam says never to do. I was judging people by what they seem to be, not what they are." He turned to Jessica with an open smile. "Adam says that next to thinking only of yourself, that's the worst thing you can do."

"Well," Jessica said carefully, "sometimes it isn't easy not to think about yourself."

"Oh, of course it isn't," Annie said. "That's why Adam wants us to devote ourselves to good works."

"Good works?" Jessica repeated.

"That's right," Ted cut in. "Not only do we help one another, but we help thousands of other people, too, by raising money for different charities. That's why Adam's so busy. He does all the organization of our charity work."

"Oh, I see," Jessica said. "That's why he needs his own room to work in." She looked over at Ted. "And that's what you were doing when I met you in the mall!"

Ted nodded. "That's right. Saturday's always a good day for collecting there."

Mary leaned toward Jessica. "Adam says it's not enough to *want* to help others. You have to actually do it."

Sky nodded. "Adam says that charitable work is the most important work there is."

"Well, I'm sure he's right," Jessica said. An image of Adam Marvel was beginning to form in her mind. He must be an older man, she reasoned, even older than her parents, with white hair and a gentle manner. He was obviously very good and very generous. She pictured him as a cross between Santa Claus and the President.

"So," Susan said, suddenly entering the conversation, "do you think you're going to join the group, Jessica?"

Jessica was caught completely off guard. After all, she had come only for supper, not to move in. "Oh, well . . . I . . . uh . . . I don't think so," she mumbled. The others were looking at her expectantly. She was sure that they were wondering how anyone could not want to live such a good and happy life. "I don't think I could share a room like you all do," she explained. "I need my privacy."

Susan eyed her coldly. "The only people who need privacy are people who have something to hide," she said evenly. A tiny smile turned up the corners of her mouth. "That's what Adam says."

As she got ready to go home Jessica decided that, all in all, the evening had not been so bad. It was the first time in a long time that she had felt genuinely appreciated and wanted. It was certainly the first time in a long time that anyone had given her as much attention as the Good Friends had.

They gathered around her as she stood by the door.

"Come back soon," Annie said. "We really enjoyed having you."

"That goes for all of us," Brian said, giving her hand a hearty shake.

Mary hugged her. "I'll be thinking of you, all alone in your room with your homework," she whispered.

"You sure you couldn't stay a little longer?" Ted asked. "I really wish you could meet Adam."

"Oh, no," Jessica said quickly. "I really should get going." She didn't explain that she wanted to get home in case Sam had been trying to get hold of her. Talking about everything had made her feel so much better that she was ready to get back to her real life.

Jessica hadn't heard a car outside, and she hadn't heard anyone on the porch. But as she turned to leave the door opened suddenly. Jessica stared in surprise. There, only a few feet away from her, was one of the most attractive men she had ever seen. Although he was obviously much older than she, he couldn't have been over thirty. He had perfect, chiseled features, piercing green eyes and thick, wavy blond hair. Dressed in an expensive blue suit and pale yellow shirt, he didn't look as though he belonged in the Good Friends' house. He looked like a model or a movie star. He was gazing straight at her, and she had the strange sensation that his incredible eyes could see right into her heart.

Without meaning to, Jessica smiled. He smiled back at her, and the whole room seemed to light up. Jessica had never seen anything like it before.

"Adam!" several people shouted. "We're so glad you're home!"

Adam? Jessica could hardly believe her ears. This couldn't be Adam Marvel. Adam Marvel was a middle-aged man in a baggy old suit. Adam Marvel was a do-gooder, and do-gooders weren't supposed to be outrageously handsome.

Adam continued to smile at her and Jessica continued to stare.

"Adam," Ted said, taking Jessica's arm and propelling her forward. "Adam, I want you to meet someone."

Adam Marvel reached out and took Jessica's hand in his own. His hand was large and strong. "Don't tell me," he said in a rich, warm voice, "this must be Jessica Wakefield, Ted told me all about you this afternoon. He was so glad he'd met you." He squeezed her hand. "I would have known you anywhere."

"Oh, same here," Jessica managed to say.

He let go of her hand, but his eyes still held her. "I hope you'll excuse me, but I have to change out of my business clothes. You weren't leaving, were you?"

Jessica let her bag fall to the floor. "Oh, no," she said quickly. "I wasn't going anywhere."

What an evening! Jessica shoved several blouses and a stack of schoolbooks onto the floor and flopped on her bed. In just a few hours, the world had turned upside down. To think that she might have gone on forever, thinking that life was all about parties and cheerleading and double-cheese pizza, if she hadn't met Adam Marvel.

Jessica closed her eyes, going over everything that had happened from the moment Adam walked into the Good Friends' house until the moment he walked her to her car.

When he had returned to the living room after changing into casual clothes—jeans and a black T-shirt—Jessica couldn't help but notice that unlike the other male members of the group, Adam had a perfect physique. They had all gathered around him while he told Jessica the story of how he had come to found the Good Friends. Although they must have heard it before, the others had all followed every syllable, just as Jessica had.

There seemed to be nothing that Adam Marvel hadn't done, and nowhere he hadn't been. Not that he had bragged or boasted. For all his good looks and charisma, it was clear to Jessica that Adam Marvel was a quiet, modest man. The others had had to drag information out of him. "Tell Jessica about the poor widow and her children you helped in New York," they had begged him. "Tell Jessica about the grape pickers you befriended in Italy."

Jessica had listened spellbound while he made the most ordinary things sound like miracles, and the most exotic things sound everyday. Sitting there beside him, she had understood why the others talked about him so much. He was a very special person. Everything about him was gentle, understanding, and kind. Adam had been the one to suggest that Jessica go home before her parents became worried.

When he had invited her to come back the next

day to help them do some work on the lawn, she immediately accepted.

Jessica began to imagine what might happen on Sunday afternoon. Adam would ask her to help him with the weeds. Only it would be a pretext. He would want to talk to her alone, to find out more about her. He would see how alone and unloved she was and befriend her. He would see that she was a very special person and understand her as no one else ever had. . . .

Jessica's happy daydream was interrupted by the sudden arrival in her room of her twin. Elizabeth burst through the door, dropping down on the bed beside Jessica with an excited shriek.

Jessica opened her eyes.

"I had the most wonderful time!" Elizabeth exclaimed. "Everyone's so nice, and Justin—that's our coach—he's amazing. I can't remember the last time I laughed so much," she continued, her eyes dancing. "Todd bounced his ball across two lanes!"

Jessica stared at her sister in disbelief. How could Elizabeth interrupt her with nonsense when she was thinking about serious things?

Elizabeth gave Jessica a nudge. "You really should join, too. It's so much fun!"

Jessica recalled the tranquility and sincerity of the Good Friends. She remembered Adam's penetrating green eyes. "Elizabeth," Jessica snapped, jumping off the bed and marching toward the bathroom, "it's about time you realized that there's a lot more to life than just having fun."

40

Four

As soon as she awoke the next morning, Jessica jumped out of bed. Usually she liked to sleep late on Sundays, but today was different. For the first time in ages, she had something important to look forward to. Not just a date, or a dance, or a new pair of shorts. Today she was going to talk to Adam again. Somehow she knew—she just knew—that he had the answer to all her problems.

Jessica pulled on her oldest pair of jeans and the shirt she wore when her mother made her clean out the garage. After all, she told herself, Adam had solved all of Ted's and Brian's problems, hadn't he? Both Sky and Mary had told her how he had changed their lives. Why shouldn't he be able to solve her problems, too? Why shouldn't he turn *her* life around? She looked at herself in the mirror. *You've got to keep this a secret*, she told herself sternly. She could just imagine how Sam and her family would laugh at her if they found out about the Good Friends. She knew exactly what they would say. "It's just another one of Jessica's phases." She could hear Elizabeth giggling. "Remember the time Jessica was going to Hawaii to meet the man of her dreams."

"She'll get over it," her mother would say. "These things never last for long."

Jessica's reflection looked back at her with a determined expression. "We'll show them," she said out loud.

She was in the kitchen before anyone else was up. Whistling a happy tune, she decided to get ready for her day with the Good Friends by practicing helping others.

By the time her mother came downstairs, Jessica had the coffee brewing and was stirring pancake batter in a large yellow bowl.

"Jessica?" Mrs. Wakefield asked, sounding confused.

"Good morning, Mom," Jessica said cheerfully.

"Jessica, what are you doing?"

"I'm making pancakes," Jessica answered, as though this were the most normal thing in the world. "Why don't you sit down? The first batch will be ready in a minute."

"Is Sam coming to breakfast?" Mrs. Wakefield asked as she obediently sat down. "He called you at least six times yesterday, you know."

Sam! Jessica groaned inwardly. She had completely forgotten about Sam. She would have to call him and tell him she had to study for English today or he might stop by.

42

"No," Jessica said, thinking quickly. "I'm spending the day with him, but he's not coming for breakfast." She gave her mother a smile. "I thought I'd surprise you, that's all."

"Well, you've certainly succeeded in doing that," Mrs. Wakefield replied.

"Doing what?" asked Elizabeth, coming into the kitchen.

Her mother nodded at Jessica, who was turning pancakes at the stove. "Surprising me by making breakfast."

Elizabeth's blue eyes widened in mock alarm. "Oh, no!" she gasped. "This is awful! The laundry monster has taken all of Jessica's clothes."

Jessica frowned. "What are you talking about, Elizabeth?"

Elizabeth, barely able to keep from laughing, pointed at her. "You're wearing *old* clothes!"

Maybe it was because it was a bright, sunny morning, and not a gray, cloudy evening, but Cedar Street didn't look as bad that day as it had the night before. It wasn't Calico Drive, with its beautiful homes and well-kept lawns, but Jessica could see that it wasn't nearly as awful as she had first thought, either.

She pulled to a stop in front of number six. Her eyes moved from the top of the house to the bottom. At the upstairs windows, the brightly patterned Indian spreads fluttered in the breeze; the wind chimes that hung from the eaves of the porch tinkled in a welcoming way. It might be a little rundown, but she had to admit that the house had a lot of character.

Feeling a little nervous, Jessica walked up the path. All the way there, she had been wondering what would happen. What if Adam had to go out on business again? What if she got stuck weeding with Susan or Annie or one of the other kids? What if he had invited her only out of politeness? What if he had forgotten who she was? Jessica climbed up the cinder block stairs. *Don't be silly*, she chided herself. *What difference does it make if Adam isn't here? You're not here to see him.* She took a deep breath. *You're here to help.* She rang the bell.

Almost immediately the door flew open and the day became ten times sunnier. Adam Marvel was home and from the smile on his face, he was happy to see her.

"Jessica!" he cried. "I'm so glad you could come." His smile became apologetic. "I was so tired last night that I must have seemed very rude. I didn't really have a chance to talk to *you* at all."

Being at a loss for words wasn't one of Jessica's usual problems, but there was something in the way he pronounced the word *you* that tied her tongue in knots. "Oh, well," she finally managed to say. "I promised I'd come."

He took her hand. "I know you did," he said. "And I should have realized you were a woman of your word, but I was foolishly afraid that you might have changed your mind."

She was sure she saw a flicker of sadness in those emerald-green eyes.

"People often do, you know," he added.

"Oh, not me," she assured him. "I always try to keep my word."

He nodded. "I have the feeling that you're a very interesting person. That's why I thought that perhaps you and I could work together today, cleaning out the garage." The green eyes twinkled. "It would give me a chance to get to know you better."

Adam Marvel wanted to work with her! Jessica couldn't believe her luck. Whenever her parents wanted her to clean out the garage, Jessica moaned and groaned about getting dirty and breaking her nails. She complained for days about ruining her clothes and breathing in dust. But now all she said was, "Oh, that would be great!" She lowered her eyes. "I'm the one who takes care of our garage at home."

Jessica had never seen anything as dirty and full of junk as the Good Friends' garage. It was so crowded with old tires, stacks of paper, and broken furniture, it was a wonder there was enough room to park the group's van. It made Jessica's room at home—a room her sister often referred to as "The Pit"—look immaculate.

Adam whistled. "Whew. This is even worse than I thought."

But Jessica's heart soared at the sight. It was going to take them hours to clean this out!

They had just begun to make a pile of things to throw out when a shadow fell across them.

Susan was standing in the entrance, her arms folded across her chest and a suspicious look on her face. "I thought *I* was supposed to be doing this with you," she said to Adam.

With only a glance in her direction, Adam turned back to the stack of magazines he had been moving. "I changed my mind," he said shortly. "Jessica's helping me instead. I want you to work in the yard with Sky and Annie."

Susan didn't budge. "But yesterday you said you wanted *me* to do the garage."

Adam flung the magazines onto the pile with a force that surprised Jessica, but his voice, when he spoke, was as calm as ever. "And now I'm saying that I don't."

As soon as Susan had stormed off, Adam turned to Jessica with a rueful smile. "I'm sorry about that," he said quietly. "I don't want you to think that that sort of behavior is typical of the Good Friends."

"Oh, no," Jessica said quickly. "I know it's not." She lowered her voice, too. "To tell you the truth, I don't think Susan likes me very much."

Adam touched her arm. "It's not you. Believe me, it has nothing to do with you. All anyone could talk about last night was how much they liked you." He hesitated for a few seconds before going on. Jessica could tell that he was trying to find the right words to explain the situation and be fair at the same time. "The problem with Susan is that she's just joined the group. Sometimes it takes people a little while before they forget about their old, selfish behavior and learn how to be a Good Friend." He shook his head. "To be honest, Jessica, I don't think Susan's totally settled into our ways yet."

Jessica nodded wisely. Being as pretty and popular as she was—and as flirtatious as she used to be—she had seen enough girls behave as Susan just had to know exactly what was wrong. "You mean she has a crush on you?"

Adam's face lit up with wonder and relief. "I don't believe you! You're even more mature and understanding than I thought!" Impulsively, he gave her a hug. "Ted was right about you. He said you were really special, and you certainly are."

Jessica felt herself go pink with pleasure at his praise. "Ted was right about you, too."

It had never occurred to Jessica before that work could actually be enjoyable. But working with Adam was so much fun that the morning turned into afternoon, and the afternoon into late afternoon, before she knew it. Working with people for a common cause was fun, just as Adam said it was. In fact, everything that Adam told her while they were alone together made sense. He asked her questions about herself and listened to her tell her story, and then he made her see things in a different light.

"You see, Jessica," Adam said as he walked her to her car at the end of the day, "being part of a group—really belonging to a group—is one of the greatest experiences a person can have."

"Well, I have always liked being a cheerleader,"

Jessica said. "Until recently, anyway. And I'm proud to belong to Pi Beta Alpha."

"That's not exactly what I meant," he said in his gentle way. "Admit it, Jessica. When you're doing your cheers, or organizing a sorority dance, don't you want to be the *best* cheerleader or the most popular Pi Beta Alpha?"

"Well, everybody does," Jessica defended herself.

Adam shook his head with an understanding smile. "Don't you see, Jessica? As long as you feel like that, you're not really part of the group. You're *competing* with the group."

Jessica could only stare at him in awe. He was right! She had only been thinking of herself, not the group as a whole. "I never thought about it like that before," she confessed.

"Of course you haven't," Adam said. They reached the Fiat. "Our society teaches us to think only of the individual." He lowered his voice. "You know, I've been watching you today, and I can tell that you were more comfortable and relaxed than you have been in a long time." He stared directly into her eyes. "Am I right?"

Jessica nodded.

He stepped back as she got into the car. "You know what I think, Jessica? I think that's because we bring out the best in you. Because we really appreciate you."

"Oh, you do," she agreed. "You really do."

"We never demand things from our friends," Adam continued. "We believe that people should be themselves." He leaned toward her.

"It's obvious from what you've told me today that the people you usually associate with are selfish and self-centered. Because they're that way, they make you that way, too. You have no opportunity to express your true nature which is giving and generous."

Jessica nodded. Of course she had no opportunity to express her true nature when everyone was always criticizing her and telling her what to do. Not when people like Lila Fowler were always trying to make Jessica feel inferior because she didn't buy her clothes in Paris and couldn't visit London whenever she wanted.

Jessica stared up at Adam. "You know, I never thought of that before, either."

"The Good Friends are good friends to everyone," Adam said. "Don't forget that. Instead of shrinking inside of themselves, they reach out and help. Helping others is the only way we can really help ourselves." Even in the fading afternoon light, his smile was bright.

Jessica sighed out loud. "That's one of the most profound things I've ever heard."

Adam leaned a little closer. "We really want to help you, Jessica. We think you have the potential to be an exceptionally fine person, and we'd very much like you to be our friend."

Jessica tingled with joy. "And I'd like to be your friend, too."

When she had spoken to Sam earlier that day, Jessica had agreed to go to the movies with him that night. "I don't want you to be mad at me," Sam had said. "I want things to go back to the way they were."

All through the film, Jessica sat holding Sam's hand and thinking about the way things were. Lately that meant Jessica sitting by herself in a room with a pile of homework and Sam out enjoying himself on his bike. *But even before that, things weren't so great,* Jessica told herself.

Sam passed her the popcorn. *This,* thought Jessica, *is a perfect example of what things have been like.* Sam knew she didn't like popcorn, but did he care? No. He liked popcorn, so every time they went to a movie, he bought popcorn. And every time, he ate it himself!

It was just as Adam had said: people were selfish.

She shoved the popcorn back to him.

"How about a post-film snack at the Dairi Burger?" Sam asked as they filed out of the theater.

Since lunch at the Good Friends' house that afternoon had, in fact, consisted of tofu and steamed vegetables, a meal that wasn't exactly one of Jessica's favorites, she couldn't quite resist the idea of a cheeseburger and fries. "OK," she said reluctantly, "if you insist."

A lot of their friends were already there. Jessica and Sam joined April Dawson, Michael Harris, Maria Santelli, Winston Egbert, Lila, Amy, Aaron Dallas, Rose Jameson, and Eddie Strong at one of the back tables.

"Gee," Amy said to Jessica as she sat down,

"it's been so long since I've seen you out at night that I almost didn't recognize you."

Lila grabbed Jessica's hand. "What's happened to your nails?" she asked. "The polish is chipped."

Jessica tossed her head. "I've been working."

"I'd stop that right away if I were you, Jessica," Winston teased her. "You're going to ruin your reputation."

Jessica frowned. Were these the people she had thought were funny and interesting? Was this the sort of evening she had been missing while she was grounded? Sitting squashed in a booth while everyone talked and shouted and laughed at once?

While the others chatted happily, Jessica sat back and listened to their conversations. The boys talked about nothing but sports and music; the girls talked about nothing but clothes and gossip. They were so shallow. They never thought about anyone but themselves. Adam Marvel's voice ran through her mind. *The people you usually associate with are selfish and self-centered, but you have the potential to be exceptional. You are special.*

"What's the matter, Jess?" Sam asked as he stopped his car in front of her house later that night. He reached for her hand. "You've been so quiet all night."

Jessica continued to stare out the window. "I've been thinking."

"What about?" he joked. "What you're going to wear to April's party next week?"

Jessica turned to him coldly. "No," she replied

51

in a tight, distant voice. "I wasn't. As a matter of fact, I'm not even sure I can go to April's party."

Even in the darkness of the car, she could see his surprise. "What do you mean, you can't go?" he asked. "I thought you were really looking forward to it. I thought you were going to help me improve my dancing."

"I have more important things to do with my life than dance." Jessica opened the car door and stepped onto the pavement. "Unlike you," she added as she slammed it shut behind her.

"I always liked bowling," Elizabeth said as she and Todd sat down at a corner table at Guido's, "but I never realized it could be this much fun."

They had just come from The Fast Lane, the local bowling alley, where the Sweet Valley High team had had its first official practice. Everyone had had so much fun, they'd stayed two hours longer than they'd planned.

"It's all right for those of us who happen to be the teacher's pet," Todd said with mock seriousness, "but some of us really had to work out there." He rubbed his arm. "Those balls are pretty heavy when you don't have some six-foot champion bowler helping you hold it."

"Why, Todd Wilkins!" Elizabeth said, laughing. "Just what are you suggesting?"

"Me?" asked Todd innocently. "I'm not suggesting anything. All I'm saying is that Justin seemed to spend a lot more time showing you how to position yourself than he did showing anyone else."

"The only reason he devoted so much time to helping me is because I need so much help," Elizabeth said.

"Oh, sure, Elizabeth, and that probably explains why Justin had to grab you every time he wanted you to move your feet a quarter of an inch."

"Don't be silly," Elizabeth said, taking hold of his hand. She stared deeply into his eyes. "Todd, I want you to know that even though Justin is incredibly handsome, smart, funny, and charming, I still love you."

Five

Elizabeth lay in bed the next Saturday morning long after her alarm had sounded. The past week had been a hectic one for her, so she was content to lie there for a while, listening to Jessica singing in the shower.

Elizabeth yawned. Besides homework, a science field trip, and her weekly column for *The Oracle*, she had had to practice for the bowling team as well.

Elizabeth smiled to herself as she climbed out of bed. Her eyes fell on the pink-and-green badge that she had left on her desk: Bowl Till You Drop. Justin had given one to each of them as a joke. Elizabeth stared at the badge thinking about the bowling team: the hard work, fun, and Justin Silver. She gave herself a little shake. *Don't be silly*, she scolded herself. *No matter what Todd says, Justin is only interested in you as a bowler*. The pin seemed to fade away, and she found herself thinking about Justin's humorous gray eyes. She could feel his arms around her, showing her how to position her body. She could hear his voice. "You're too much, Ms. Wakefield. Brains, beauty, *and* a first-class bowler. I wish I'd met you before Wilkins did."

Elizabeth gave herself another shake. *And you're only interested in him as a coach*, she reminded herself. She turned sharply toward the bathroom. The sound of Jessica's singing had stopped. Elizabeth glanced at her clock. What was going on? Here it was eight-thirty on a Saturday morning, and not only was she thinking of a boy other than Todd, but Jessica had been *singing in the shower*. Elizabeth shook her head in amazement. Most Saturdays, Jessica didn't even *speak* until noon.

A little while later Elizabeth went down to breakfast, expecting Jessica to be sitting at the table, but her place was still empty. "Isn't Jessica down yet?" she asked in surprise. "I know she's up."

Mrs. Wakefield looked up from her paper with a knowing smile. "Up is not the same as dressed," she said.

"That's right." Mr. Wakefield grinned. "It could be another day and a half before Jessica surfaces."

"Did I hear my name?" Jessica asked as she came into the kitchen. Elizabeth was immediately struck by Jessica's outfit—a severe brown skirt and a plain white cotton blouse. Her hair was tied back with a brown velvet ribbon.

Elizabeth and her mother exchanged a look.

Over the years, the family had seen Jessica in a number of different guises, from rock star to saleswoman, but they had never seen her looking quite like this before. *No wonder it took Jessica so long to get dressed,* Elizabeth thought. *She must have had to dig through everything she owns to find that outfit.*

"Are you trying out for the role of librarian in the school play or something?" Mr. Wakefield joked.

Jessica gave him a withering look as she slipped into her chair. "No," she said evenly, helping herself to some cereal. "I just felt like looking a little calmer than usual today."

Elizabeth's eyes fell on the box of cereal in her sister's hand. "Jessica," she said, "that's muesli you're pouring into your bowl."

It was Elizabeth's turn to receive a withering look. "I can read, you know," Jessica snapped. "I may not win prizes for my journalism, Elizabeth Wakefield, but I can tell the difference between cornflakes and muesli."

Elizabeth's eyes sparkled with mischief. "I thought you said muesli tastes like horse food."

Jessica had, in fact, compared muesli to hay a number of times. It ranked next to tofu in her list of least favorite foods.

"I never said any such thing," Jessica replied. "I think you must be confusing me with someone else."

Elizabeth decided to let it pass. She took a deep breath and began again. "Todd and I were wondering if you and Sam wanted to come bowling with us this afternoon," she said brightly. "We thought it might be fun."

"Fun?" Jessica raised one eyebrow and gazed at her sister as though *fun* were a nasty word. "I don't have time for fun. I have a lot of studying to do in the library today. I'm not sure what time I'll be back."

"But you've been working so hard all week," Mrs. Wakefield said.

"I thought you were concerned about my grades," Jessica said. "I thought you'd be happy that I was going to spend the day studying." She put a small spoonful of muesli into her mouth. Elizabeth couldn't tell from the expression on her face whether she intended to swallow it or spit it out.

Mrs. Wakefield sighed. "Of course I'm happy," she answered. "It's just that you've been at the library almost every evening this week. I like to see you enjoy yourself, too."

"Me, too," Jessica agreed. "That's why I don't think I want to go bowling with Todd and Elizabeth. Wasting time isn't always the same thing as enjoying yourself, you know."

"Wasting time?" Elizabeth exclaimed.

But Jessica was pushing her cereal bowl away. "Speaking of time," she said, jumping to her feet, "I have to get going. I had no idea it was so late."

The rest of the family stared after her as she hurried out the kitchen door.

"Is this a new phase?" Mr. Wakefield asked. "Conservative clothes, muesli, studying all the time . . ."

Alice Wakefield shook her head. "It certainly seems to be."

Elizabeth gazed thoughtfully at the kitchen door. Scenes from the past week were flashing through her mind. Jessica missing meals because she had to study. Jessica sitting with her friends at lunch gazing off into space instead of talking animatedly, as she usually did. Jessica wearing subdued colors. Elizabeth had been so busy herself lately that she hadn't been paying much attention to her twin. But something was definitely up.

Jessica tossed her books into the back of the car, and glanced at her watch again as she started up the Fiat. She didn't normally wear a watch, but Adam had suggested it so she wouldn't be late for Good Friends activities. Jessica could still taste that one extraordinarily unpleasant spoonful of muesli, but she didn't have time to stop for a doughnut on the way. She knew how important punctuality was to Adam. It had taken her ages to put her boring outfit together. Adam said that people were more willing to give money to people they didn't think were frivolous.

Contrary to what she had told her parents, Jessica was going to help the Good Friends collect money for worthy causes. It was the least she could do, she reasoned. She had been spending most of her free time with them recently and was really beginning to feel like a valued member of the group.

"Hi there!" Jessica called as she strode into the Good Friends' kitchen. She was so at home with them now that she didn't even have to knock at the door. She just walked right in.

Adam, Brian, Ted, Annie, and Susan were sitting around the table, finishing their breakfasts. They all looked up.

Adam smiled. "Well, if it isn't our own little ray of sunshine."

To hide her pleasure at this compliment, Jessica pointed to the bowl of muesli he was eating. "That's what I had this morning, too."

"See how well you fit in with us?" Ted said.

"I guess I do," Jessica said happily, sitting down between him and Brian.

Annie stared at her from across the table. "I love the way you're dressed," she said in her quiet, earnest voice. "You look so mature."

"It's very becoming," Adam said softly. "Very becoming. I think this thoughtful, old-fashioned side of you is one you've been afraid to express before."

Susan pushed back her chair with a harsh, scraping sound. "You certainly don't look like a cheerleader anymore," she snapped. She looked at Adam. "I think I'll go wait in the van."

Adam nodded. "Suit yourself." He turned to Jessica. "We're breaking up into small groups for today." He gestured around the table. "I thought you could join my group for your first outing. That way I can explain the procedure to you on the drive over."

Jessica felt a warm rush of happiness flow

59

through her. This was even better than she had hoped. She would be with Adam all day. He would see for himself how sincere and hardworking Jessica could be.

As they drove, Adam explained they were going to the neighboring town of Palisades to collect money door to door. He talked about what a good time they would have.

A little to her surprise, Jessica soon discovered that Adam was right. The time seemed to fly by. The more she collected, the better she seemed to get at it. People genuinely seemed to like and trust her. When she explained the work the Good Friends did, they listened patiently instead of slamming the door in her face, as she had half expected they would.

"Well," said one woman, after hearing Jessica's speech about helping others and making the world a better place, "I don't believe much in these things myself, but I can see that you do. You're a very fine young lady." She smiled. "I'll give you a donation because I'm so impressed with you."

Adam was impressed with Jessica, too. "I don't believe it!" he cried as they sat in the van at the end of the afternoon, doing a quick assessment of what they had taken in. "It's only her first time, and it feels to me from shaking her box that Jessica's collected more than anyone else." He patted her shoulder. "Good work. I knew you had it in you."

Jessica couldn't believe how good she felt. And

how proud that she had done something to benefit others. Adam was right. The Good Friends
were bringing out the best in her!

On the ride home, while the group was sitting
in the back of the van, singing, Adam suddenly
pulled into a supermarket parking lot.

"What's up?" Susan asked as they came to a
stop.

Adam opened one of the money canisters.
"Brian and I are going to do a little shopping."
He removed a handful of bills from the box and
put back the lid. "I don't know about you guys,"
he said with a grin, "but I am starving. Doing
good deeds makes me hungry."

Jessica was so surprised by this that it took her
a few moments to respond. Brian was already
climbing over her to get out of the van when she
suddenly found her voice. "Wait a minute!" she
protested. "You can't spend that money."

A heavy silence fell over the group.

"I—I don't mean to sound critical," Jessica
stammered, all at once feeling unsure of herself.
"But we didn't collect it for us. We collected it for
the needy."

"That's one of the things I like best about you,
Jessica," Adam said, giving her one of his most
dazzling smiles. "You're a woman of real principles. You have an instinctive selflessness in you—
that's why you did so well today." He leaned
across the seat and patted her shoulder. "But this
is completely legitimate," he assured her.

Jessica looked around. The others were nodding in agreement with Adam.

"After all," he continued, "we have to have some to cover our expenses—food and things like that—or we wouldn't be able to continue doing the job we do. If we had to go out and work to earn money for ourselves, we wouldn't have enough time to devote to all the charities we support."

Jessica found it difficult to think and meet Adam's emerald gaze at the same time, but she did have to admit that what he said made sense. "Well," she said, "when you put it that way . . ."

"Trust me," Adam said. "You know I wouldn't do anything that's wrong."

Every head in the van nodded in agreement, Jessica's included.

But as soon as Adam and Brian left the van, Susan turned to Jessica. "Maybe this isn't the group for you if you're going to argue with Adam," she said with a hard, tight smile.

"Oh, Jessica wasn't arguing with Adam," Annie broke in. "Were you, Jessica?"

Jessica shook her head. "No, of course I wasn't. I just didn't understand."

"Do you understand now?" Susan pushed, not taking her eyes from Jessica's face.

"Oh, Susan," pleaded Annie, suddenly looking frightened. "Let's not have any trouble, all right? I hate trouble. I really do."

"Don't we all?" asked Susan, still looking at Jessica.

When Adam and Brian returned in good spirits, with bags of food, Susan acted as though nothing had happened. For the rest of the journey, they munched on potato chips and sang songs. And, despite the interruption, Adam's group was the first to return to the house.

"How about you girls fixing us something to eat while the boys and I sort out the money into bills and change?" suggested Adam as they all scrambled out of the van.

"Not me," Susan said quickly. "If I don't get a shower, I'll die." She tugged at her T-shirt. "Doing good deeds can be dirty work."

Jessica could see that this was a chance for her to get herself back in Adam's favor, and maybe score some points with the rest of the Good Friends as well. "I'll do it," she volunteered.

Annie linked her arm in hers. "And I'll help," she said.

Jessica had never really been alone with Annie before. Watching her bustle around the kitchen, humming a cheerful tune, it was hard to imagine her ever being unhappy. *And yet she must have had problems in her life, or she wouldn't be here*, Jessica thought.

"Annie," she said, almost thinking out loud, "I hope you won't think I'm being nosy, but why did you join the Good Friends?"

"Oh, I don't think you're being nosy," said Annie in her soft, breathless voice. A bright pink color came into her cheeks. She looked down at her hands. "The day I met Adam was the best day of my life," she whispered excitedly.

"Were you unhappy before that?" Jessica asked.

Annie glanced at her shyly, blushing even

more. "I was an only child," she said, turning her attention to the lettuce she was shredding. "And my parents fought all the time."

Jessica nodded sympathetically. She could remember a period when her own parents had fought all the time. It had been terrible.

"When they weren't yelling at each other, they were yelling at me," Annie explained. "I was so miserable! I felt like everything was my fault, that I couldn't do anything right."

"I know what that's like," said Jessica with feeling.

"So I ran away," Annie whispered. "I don't know what I thought I was going to do. I had no money and no friends. But I just couldn't stand it a second longer." She raised her eyes, a look of joy coming to her face. "That's when Adam found me," she explained. "He's the most wonderful person I've ever met. He completely changed my life." She leaned toward Jessica. "I used to feel so bad about myself, but now I know I'm as good as anyone."

"Adam seems to affect everyone that way," said Jessica. She tossed a handful of carrot slices into the salad bowl. She never felt better about herself than when she was with Adam and the Good Friends. "What about when you're not with the group?" Jessica asked. "How do you feel then?"

"But I'm always with the group," she answered instantly. "Adam doesn't really like us to associate with people from outside."

Jessica was shocked. Before she could respond,

Adam himself strolled into the room. "What Annie means," he said cheerfully, not hiding the fact that he had overheard them, "is that we've learned through experience that outsiders don't always understand us or our ways." He turned his smile on Jessica.

She couldn't help smiling back.

"You know how easy it is for people to misunderstand you," Adam continued. "How easy it is for them to accuse you of things you never did or intended."

Jessica nodded. She certainly did! Wasn't that what was always happening to her?

"People are always looking for someone else to take the blame," Adam said. He gave Jessica a significant look. "Especially if you're a little special, a little different from what's considered normal."

"Oh, yes," she said, "I know exactly what you mean."

Adam picked a slice of carrot from the salad and popped it into his mouth with a conspiratorial wink. "That's why we like to keep to ourselves as much as possible," he said. "The less you say to outsiders about us, the better off we'll all be." He put an arm around Annie and gave her a hug. "Isn't that right, Annie? You wouldn't want to have to go back to your parents, would you?"

Annie shook her head vehemently. "I'd rather go to jail." She leaned against him. "Of course you're right," she said quietly. "You're always right."

"Jessica?" asked Adam, putting his other arm around her.

"Of course," Jessica agreed.

"What do you mean, you're too tired to go?" Sam was standing in the Wakefields' hallway, a bunch of flowers in his hand and a bewildered expression on his face. He had arrived at eight o'clock to take Jessica to April's party, but not only was she not ready, she had forgotten all about it.

"I told you last week I might not go," Jessica said. "Why don't you pay attention to anything I say?"

Sam waved the flowers in the air. "That was last week," he argued. "You didn't say anything about not going when I talked to you last night."

Jessica tossed her head. "Last night I hadn't spent the entire day in the library studying for an English test."

"That's another thing," Sam said. "Elizabeth said you'd gone to the library, so I stopped by to take you to lunch, but you weren't there."

The color drained from Jessica's face for just a moment. Stretching the truth might be wrong when you were doing it for personal reasons, but not when you were doing it for a good cause, as she was now. What better cause was there than protecting Adam and the Good Friends from outsiders who didn't understand? Her eyes flashed. "Were you spying on me?" she asked darkly. "You don't even trust me, you have to go sneaking around town after me?"

Sam looked horrified. "Of course I wasn't spying on you. I just wanted to surprise you."

"Oh, sure," Jessica said. "So you followed me all the way to the Cold Springs library."

"Cold Springs?" he repeated. "Why did you go there? I thought you'd be in Sweet Valley."

"That's why I'm so tired," Jessica explained. "They didn't have the books I needed in Sweet Valley." She sighed dramatically. "Here I am trying so hard to prove to my parents that I can do well in school, and instead of being supportive you treat me like I'm some sort of criminal."

"I'm sorry, Jess," Sam said. "I really am. It's just that I've missed you so much. It feels like we haven't been together in weeks."

He started to put his arms around her, but she pushed him away. "And whose fault is that?" she demanded. "You prefer to spend time with your dirt bike rather than with me."

"Look," Sam said, "I don't want to argue, OK? Let's not fight about whose fault it is. Let's just spend some time together." His face brightened. "I know," he said with a smile. "Why don't we order a pizza and stay in and watch TV tonight?"

The idea of curling up on the couch with Sam and a pepperoni pizza was so familiar and so pleasant that for a moment Jessica almost relented. But the truth was that not only was she exhausted, she also wanted some time to herself. As she was leaving the Good Friends that evening, Adam had stopped her to congratulate her again on all the money she had raised. "You're a wonder," he had told her. "A real wonder." Jessica wanted to be alone so she could close her eyes and hear him saying that over and over.

"Well?" Sam asked. "Double cheese with jalapeño peppers?"

"I don't eat pizza with a person who doesn't trust me," Jessica said coolly. "Why don't you go watch TV with your bike?"

Six

Elizabeth had just settled down at her desk on Monday night when the telephone rang. Much to her surprise, it was Justin Silver. Although the group had broken up much earlier that afternoon, it sounded as though he was still in the bowling alley. She could hear the sound of falling pins in the background.

"Justin?" she asked. "What's up? Did I leave something behind?"

"Uh, no," Justin said, not sounding at all like his usual confident and funny self. "No, Liz, you didn't leave anything behind. It's just that . . . well, there's something I have to talk to you about. I've been sitting here, thinking about it, and I just can't keep quiet any longer."

"Don't tell me," she joked. "You think I should take up tennis."

69

Justin laughed. "You know that's not it," he said. "You're one of the best players we have."

"It's the new uniforms, isn't it? Todd and I were talking about some ideas to raise money—"

Justin cut her short with a rush of words. "Elizabeth, the problem is not the uniforms. The problem is that I want to go out with you. I thought maybe you and I could go to the movies sometime."

Elizabeth couldn't help thinking that he was mistaken. Boys were always falling for Jessica, but not for her.

After a few moments of awkward silence, Justin said, sounding like he was gaining confidence as he spoke. "I know you and Wilkins have been together for a long time, and I'm not trying to make any trouble or anything, but I just had to ask." He laughed again, this time self-consciously. "Just in case, you know?"

"I'm really flattered, Justin," Elizabeth said, recovering from her amazement. She was glad he couldn't see her blushing. "I like you a lot, I really do. But, I can't go out with you. As you said, Todd and I have been together a long time, and we're planning to stay that way."

Justin made a sound somewhere between a laugh and a groan. "I thought you'd say that."

"Listen, Justin," Elizabeth said. "I really value our friendship."

"Me, too," Justin said softly. "Well, see you at practice, then."

After he hung up, Elizabeth went over to the mirror. She grinned at her reflection. "Well," she said out loud, "maybe you're not so dull and unexciting after all."

"Talk about teacher's pet," Todd said. It was Thursday afternoon, and he, Elizabeth, and Enid were sitting together in the cafeteria, finishing their lunches. Todd turned to Enid. "You should see Justin," he told her. "If Elizabeth hit *him* with the ball, he'd applaud her technique!"

"Oh, please," Elizabeth said, laughing, hoping she sounded a little more casual than she felt— and wishing she could change the subject. "You're exaggerating slightly." Somehow, she hadn't managed to tell Todd about Justin's phone call on Monday night.

At first she had thought that since they had gotten everything out in the open, Justin would probably completely forget about his infatuation with her. What sense did it make to upset Todd over nothing? But they had had another bowling practice on Wednesday afternoon, and Justin had been even more attentive and full of praise for her than ever. Elizabeth couldn't help feeling a little guilty. She was not, of course, doing anything to encourage Justin, but the other part of her reason for not telling Todd was that she was more flattered by Justin's attention than she wanted to admit.

"You may kid about it, Elizabeth Wakefield," Todd said in mock seriousness. "But I'm really getting worried that you're going to leave me for our bowling instructor."

Fortunately, Enid chose that moment to change

the subject. She turned to Elizabeth. "Speaking of leaving," she said, "where's Jessica? I haven't seen her since early this morning."

Elizabeth followed Enid's gaze over to where Amy, Lila, Jean West, and Sandra Bacon were sitting. The seat usually occupied by her twin was empty. "She's been studying very hard lately," Elizabeth said thoughtfully. "Maybe she's working in the library."

Enid broke a cookie in half. "That sure doesn't sound like Jessica."

"Well . . ." Elizabeth said slowly. "She's been acting a little strangely lately. Not only is she spending hours in the library studying, she's even beginning to dress differently."

Enid's eyes widened. "You mean that tweed skirt and sweater she was wearing the other day were for real?" she spluttered. "I thought it must be some sorority stunt."

"Nope," Elizabeth said, "that was the new Jessica Wakefield, serious scholar."

"I give it three days," Todd said, pushing his tray away. "Jessica's phases never last much longer than that."

Later, as they were leaving the cafeteria, Enid gave Elizabeth a nudge. Sitting on a bench at the far end of the lawn, reading a book, was Jessica. She was wearing a plain white blouse and a straight gray skirt. "Good grief," Enid hissed, "she looks like a social worker."

"I can't believe it," Elizabeth whispered back. "She really is taking this studying thing seriously."

Todd put his arm around her. "I wouldn't get too worried. It's probably a book on makeup."

Lila and Amy were leaving Sweet Valley High together that afternoon after a committee meeting for the upcoming junior dance when Sam's car pulled to a stop in front of them.

"Hi!" he called cheerfully. "Is Jessica still inside?"

Lila and Amy stared at him blankly. "Inside where?" Lila asked.

"At the meeting," Sam said. "She told me she'd be there. I thought I'd surprise her by picking her up."

Lila raised one perfect eyebrow. "Well, I guess you've surprised her, all right. She never turned up for the meeting."

"She never turned up?" Sam echoed.

Lila and Amy exchanged a look.

Lila nodded. "That's right. She said she was too busy."

"Busy?" Sam repeated. Jessica had been "busy" an awful lot lately. Every time he suggested doing something together, Jessica was "busy." "What about Sunday?" he asked, trying to sound casual. "Did she make the Pi Beta thing?"

Lila had a fixed smile on her face. "She was busy."

Sam turned to Amy. "And Tuesday night? Wasn't there some fundraiser for the cheerleaders?"

Amy glanced at Lila out of the corner of her eye. "Tuesday? Gee, I can't remember Tuesday."

73

"You went shopping with me Tuesday night," Lila interrupted. She turned to Sam with a look of concern. "We asked Jessica to go, but she was busy."

"I don't understand," he mumbled. "What's going on?"

Lila leaned against his car. "Oh, I'm sure there's some perfectly good explanation for all of this. I mean, Jessica's never been very good at staying with one person for very long. But that was before she met you." Lila pitched forward as Sam started the engine and abruptly pulled away from the curb.

"Maybe you shouldn't have said that," Amy said, catching hold of Lila's arm.

Lila straightened up. "If Jessica wants us to cover for her, then she should spend time with us again, instead of sitting by herself at lunch," Lila said huffily. "Did you see that book she was reading today? *How to Be a Better You!* I mean, have you ever heard anything so silly? Pi Betas are already perfect. How could any of us possibly improve?"

Jessica was surprised to see Sam's car parked in front of the house when she got home from the Good Friends late that afternoon. *I told him I couldn't see him today,* she said to herself as she stopped the Fiat in the driveway. Jessica started to open her door, but it was opened for her.

"Sam!" she exclaimed, trying to look pleased. "I wasn't expecting to see you."

74

"At least I know *that's* true," Sam said. It was clear he was trying to keep a hold on his temper. "Where have you been, Jessica? I've been waiting here for over an hour."

Jessica climbed out of the car. She really didn't feel like having a fight with Sam now. She had been in such a good mood after spending the afternoon with Adam, discussing the book he had loaned her, *How to Be a Better You*. He'd had so many insights to share with her that she could tell she was improving already. "I told you," Jessica said flatly. "I had a committee meeting."

"No you didn't," Sam corrected her, anger coming through in his voice. "I stopped by school to meet you, but Lila and Amy said you hadn't turned up."

Jessica started walking toward the house. *Trust Lila and Amy to betray me!* "Oh, not that committee," she said vaguely, starting to hurry a little. "This was for something else."

Sam grabbed her arm. "Jessica, you've been lying to me for days. I want to know what's going on."

Jessica shook herself free. "Don't yell at me, Sam," she said coldly. "I'm not going to discuss anything with you while you're like this. Good friends talk things through calmly and rationally. They don't raise their voices at each other." She stared into his eyes. Jessica knew her look was as cold as her voice. "They trust each other; they don't demand things."

"How can I trust you?" Sam shouted. "You tell

me you're doing one thing and you do something else. You're too busy to see me most of the time. "You—"

Jessica stamped her foot. "Who do you think you are?" she yelled back. "If you really cared about me, you wouldn't go around checking up on me. You'd let me be myself."

Sam ran his hand through his hair. "Where are you getting this stuff, Jessica? This isn't you talking. You don't sound the same, you don't even dress the same anymore. It's like aliens have taken over your body."

Adam had warned her that this would happen. He had been telling her some awful stories about members of the group whose friends and families had tried to turn them against the Good Friends. It was a good thing she had decided to keep the group a secret from everyone. She turned on her heel. "I don't want to talk to you. You're too shallow."

Sam ran beside her. "Jessica, what happened to the girl I used to go out with?" The anger in his voice had been replaced with panic. "Where is she, Jess? What's happening to you?"

She stopped so short that he walked past her. "I'm a total human being, Sam, not just some pretty girl who likes to go to parties," she yelled.

Sam threw his hands in the air. "You're a total space cadet, if you ask me." He started marching back to his car. He stopped in the middle of the driveway and turned back to her. "I don't know what's gotten into you, Jessica, but I'm going to find out!"

*   *   *

After the conversation at lunch, Elizabeth realized that she had to do something about Justin once and for all. She couldn't let things go on like this. It wasn't fair to Todd, and it wasn't fair to Justin, either. As flattered as she was by his interest, she had no intention of breaking up with Todd, and she had to make Justin accept that or she would quit the bowling group.

Full of resolve, Elizabeth arrived at the bowling alley a few minutes before the others that night.

Justin was already sitting on the bench, lacing up his shoes. He looked up when he heard her coming. "Now this is a pleasant surprise!" he called. An enormous grin spread over his handsome face. "You're not only early, you're by yourself."

There was something about his smile that made it impossible not to return it. "I have to talk to you, Justin," Elizabeth said, dropping her things down beside him. "That's why I came early."

He patted the bench beside him. "Please," he said, "sit down." His smile showed no sign of letting up. "You can talk to me all night. I hope it's something good."

Elizabeth shrugged. *This is just awful. He's so nice, and I'm enjoying the team so much. He's worked so hard with all of us. . . .* She stared at her feet. "Well, I don't know about good . . ." she began.

"Uh-oh," said Justin, his voice immediately sounding serious and worried. "Don't tell me you're leaving the team."

Elizabeth looked up in surprise. She hadn't expected him to be able to read her thoughts. "Well, no . . . I mean . . ."

He touched her arm gently. "Please, Elizabeth, I know I'm not the greatest coach in the world—"

She looked up, straight into those gray eyes. "Oh, no," she protested. "You're a wonderful coach; it isn't that. You've helped me improve my game about a hundred percent."

"Whew," he breathed, the smile returning. "You had me worried there for a second." He laughed nervously, lowering his voice. "Just being around you has improved my life about a hundred percent," he said.

Elizabeth looked down to where his hand still rested on her arm, but instead of removing it he tightened his grip. Elizabeth shook her arm free. "Justin," she said, renewing her resolve, "you have got to stop talking like that. You don't even know me. You don't know what sort of person I am, what I think is important. You just think I'm pretty."

"Beautiful," Justin whispered. "I *know* you're beautiful."

Elizabeth raised her head, her resolve returning. "That's not enough," she said firmly. "Todd and I have a real relationship. We've been through a lot together, and we know the best and the worst about each other. That's why I would never do anything to destroy what's between us."

Justin stood up, offering her his hand. "I respect and admire you for your loyalty." With a gentle tug he brought her to her feet. There were only inches between them. "I just wish it were directed at me."

Suddenly Todd's voice behind them made them both turn.

"I hope I'm interrupting something," Todd said with a smile. His tone was light, but when Elizabeth looked at him there was a question in his eyes.

Jessica was lying on her bed, still in her white blouse and gray skirt, listening to the sounds of her parents and Elizabeth talking downstairs. Although they were just in another part of the house, it felt to Jessica as though they were in another part of the world.

As if the argument with Sam had not been bad enough, Jessica's mother had overheard some of it, and had actually stuck up for him. "You can't blame him for expecting to be told the truth," Mrs. Wakefield had argued. *How typical,* Jessica had thought. *My mother doesn't care about me. She doesn't understand me. I'm always the one who's wrong!* She was so upset that after supper she made an excuse about leaving a book at Lila's and went back to the Good Friends' house to talk to Adam.

Adam, of course, had understood. Adam was on Jessica's side. Adam cared about *her*. He had explained to her that she had to expect her friends and family to behave this way. "They want you to stay the same," Adam explained. "They don't want you to reach your full potential. They find it threatening." He had told her that she was outgrowing them, just the way a snail outgrows its shell. And like the snail, she would have to find a new shell—one that was empty and waiting for her.

Jessica rolled onto her side. She knew that the new shell Adam was talking about was the Good Friends. They needed her. They were waiting for her.

She closed her eyes. Adam Marvel was smiling at her. He was telling her what a wonderful person she was. He was telling her how much she had to offer people, how much she had to offer him. Jessica opened her eyes and sat up in bed. Of course, she knew that Adam was much too old for her, but that didn't mean that he didn't care for her. They could still give each other companionship and affection.

She looked around her room. Unlike the rooms of the Good Friends, hers was a mess. It was still part of the old, party-loving, frivolous Jessica. It was the room of a girl whose friends were all shallow and insincere. If she ever did decide to live with the Good Friends, she would have to be more self-disciplined, that was for sure.

Without a second thought Jessica hurled herself from the bed and began straightening up. *If I'm going to reach my full potential, I might as well start now*, she told herself.

She was so engrossed in her task that she didn't hear Elizabeth come into the room.

"Jessica!" her twin cried in disbelief. "What are you doing?"

Jessica looked up. "What does it look like I'm doing? I'm cleaning my room."

Elizabeth grinned. "But it hasn't even been a month since the last time Mom made you clean it," she teased. "Is something wrong?"

The old, fun-loving, frivolous Jessica would have joked back. The new Jessica just stared. "I'd appreciate it if you'd leave," the new Jessica said stiffly. "I'm very busy right now."

"Well, pardon me," Elizabeth said. "I didn't mean to interrupt."

"Of course I pardon you." Jessica looked at her seriously. "Forgiveness is one of the greatest virtues," she said, quoting Adam Marvel.

"Well, I'm glad," Elizabeth said. "Because if you keep acting like this, you're going to need it."

Seven

After a restless night and a lot of thought, Elizabeth decided that Friday would be the day. She and Todd had some errands to run in town. It was the perfect opportunity to tell him about Justin.

I don't know how Jessica used to manage to juggle more than one boy at a time, Elizabeth was thinking as she waited for Todd in front of Sweet Valley High.

She knew now that quitting the bowling team wouldn't solve her problems. She smiled wryly to herself. Not that she had been very successful in her attempt to quit, and she would still have had to tell Todd why. Then he would have been upset because she hadn't confided in him. Elizabeth shook her head. He had to know what was going on. Then she would tell Justin that Todd knew everything, and things would go back to normal.

"Are you having an interesting conversation with yourself?" asked Todd, interrupting her thoughts.

Elizabeth blushed. "How long have you been standing there?"

He put an arm around her shoulder. "Long enough to know I'd better get you out of here and to the Dairi Burger for a restoring milkshake."

"Let's not go to the Dairi Burger," Elizabeth suggested as they walked to Todd's BMW. "Let's just go into town and do our errands. I have something I want to talk to you about."

Todd pulled open the car door with a flourish. "I'm surprised," he teased. "You seemed to be having a great time talking to yourself!"

It was Todd who actually did most of the talking on the drive to downtown Sweet Valley. "Did I tell you about the girl I saw in the mall last night?" he asked as soon as they were on the road.

"What girl?" she asked, only half paying attention. Most of her mind was occupied with figuring out how to bring up the subject of Justin.

"It was the funniest thing," Todd said. "I was just coming out of the shoe store and there she was. I actually started to call out 'Jessica!' before I realized it wasn't her."

"Who wasn't her?"

Todd gave her a nudge. "Pay attention," he teased. "The girl in the mall."

"Two Jessicas?" Elizabeth laughed, still not too sure what Todd was talking about. "I don't think the world is ready for that!"

She looked out the side window, returning to her thoughts. It wasn't Justin Silver who was bothering her as much as it was Elizabeth Wakefield. Justin was being a little more pushy than he should be, considering her relationship with Todd, but he wasn't really annoying or obnoxious. What was worrying her was her own reaction. She was enjoying his attention. She was beginning to look forward to practice because of the way Justin looked at her, and smiled at her, and brushed against her when he was showing her a step or handing her her ball.

"It wasn't that she really *looked* like Jessica," Todd explained, a thoughtful expression on his face. "But there was something about her . . . something about the way she was dressed, or the way she behaved ... ." He shook his head. "You know how Jessica has that sort of vague smile on her face all the time now?"

At the moment, Elizabeth was wearing a vague smile of her own. She brought herself back to the conversation. "What did you say this girl was doing?"

"She was collecting money." Todd pulled the car to a stop in front of the bakery. He had promised his mother he would bring home a cake for dessert.

Elizabeth grinned. "Well, she couldn't be anything like Jessica, then. Jessica doesn't collect money, she spends it."

Todd was about to say something more when suddenly Justin Silver came out of the bakery carrying a loaf of bread. His face lit up when he recognized them, and he hurried over to the car.

"Hey, imagine running into you two," he said with a grin, his look going right past Todd to rest on Elizabeth. "I hardly ever see you in natural light."

Elizabeth was speechless. She had been thinking of Justin most of the afternoon, and now suddenly to find him standing beside the car, grinning away at her, was more than she could handle.

"How's it going?" Todd asked.

Justin glanced at Todd. "OK, Wilkins. How's it going with you?" But before Todd could answer, his attention returned to Elizabeth. "You haven't forgotten practice tonight, have you?" he said to her.

Elizabeth finally found her voice. "Of course we haven't forgotten," she replied, a little more loudly than she had intended. "Have we, Todd?"

"We'll be there," Todd said shortly. He pulled the key from the ignition.

"Good," said Justin, still looking at Elizabeth. "It's not the same without you."

"I wish he'd stop calling me Wilkins," Todd grumbled as soon as Justin had gone. "That guy's really starting to annoy me." He made a face. "You'd think he'd never seen a beautiful blonde before."

"Todd," Elizabeth said, unable to resist a grin. "Don't tell me you really are jealous!"

Todd turned to her. "You bet I'm jealous," he said evenly. "I know I've been kidding about him a lot, but it's getting to be more than a joke. Does he think I'm so stupid that I can't see he's after my girlfriend?"

Elizabeth leaned over and gave him a hug. "Justin's the one who's stupid," she said. "Because there's no way in the world he could ever get your girlfriend."

Todd hugged her back. "I know that," he whispered. "I trust you completely, Liz. I know you would never do anything behind my back."

Elizabeth was grateful that her face was buried in his shoulder so he couldn't see her blush. *Did not telling him about Justin's phone call count as doing something behind his back?*

"So," Todd said as they stood at the counter, "what was it you wanted to talk to me about?"

"Oh," Elizabeth said, examining the cakes. "I guess it couldn't have been very important. I've forgotten it already!"

"Where's our librarian tonight?" Mr. Wakefield asked as he sat down to supper. "Don't tell me she's working late again."

Alice Wakefield passed Elizabeth the salad. "No. Tonight must be her night off. She's eating at Lila's."

Ned Wakefield helped himself to some of the casserole. "It's too bad Jessica isn't employed by the library," he said with a grin. "She'd be making a fortune and could pay for her own clothes."

Mrs. Wakefield turned to Elizabeth. "Is it my imagination, or has something drastic happened to Jessica's wardrobe lately?"

"Enid and I were just talking about that," Elizabeth answered. "Enid thinks Jessica's dressing like a social worker."

Mr. Wakefield shrugged. "Well, there are a lot worse things than that."

"Not for Jessica," Elizabeth pointed out. "She always said she'd rather be dead than drab."

But her father was shaking his head, his thoughts on something else. "Something really interesting came up at work. Did I tell you about that new group in town?" he asked, looking at his wife.

"Group?" Alice Wakefield repeated.

"They call themselves the Good Friends. They're supposed to be one of these communities that are built on love and understanding. They spend all their time raising money for different charities."

"What's wrong with that?" Elizabeth cut in. "Love and understanding and working for charity seem all right to me."

Mr. Wakefield pointed a piece of bread in her direction. "In theory, yes. No one has any trouble with that. But there are a lot of rumors going around town that not all of the charities this group says it works for are registered. And several of the reputable charities that *are* registered say they've never heard of the Good Friends. In fact," he explained, "my law firm has been asked to investigate the Good Friends by several charitable organizations who think their names are being used by the group to make money for itself."

"But isn't that illegal?" Mrs. Wakefield asked.

Ned Wakefield nodded. "Of course it's illegal. And that's not all."

Elizabeth was leaning forward. "What else could there be?"

Mr. Wakefield put his fork down. "Apparently the man who runs the Good Friends—Adam Marvel, as he calls himself—is quite a manipulator. We can't prove anything yet, but we have suspicions that Mr. Marvel has been setting up his group all over the country under different names." Mr. Wakefield cleared his throat. "Some people even think he may be starting a cult."

"A cult!" Elizabeth gasped. "Here? In Sweet Valley? But that's impossible."

Mrs. Wakefield shook her head. "I can't believe people here are gullible enough to fall for something like that."

Mr. Wakefield looked from his daughter to his wife. "Let's hope you're right," he said.

By sticking close to the other members of the team, and only speaking to Justin about pace, spin, and gutter balls, Elizabeth managed to get through bowling practice without compromising her principles. In fact, she almost managed to forget how strained things had become. The only moment of real discomfort came after practice. Todd was kidding around, helping her on with her shoes, when she happened to look up and catch Justin's eye. He was watching them with such an open and pained expression on his face that she realized that for all his bravado, he really was serious about her. Todd had been right: it was a lot more than a joke.

"I was glad to see Justin keeping his mind on the game a little more than usual," Todd said as they found themselves a table at the Dairi Burger. He looked a little sheepish. "Maybe I overreacted a little."

"Don't worry about it," Elizabeth said.

Todd shook his head. "No, I really let him get to me this afternoon, and I'm sorry." He reached across the table to take her hand. "I wouldn't want you to think I'm one of these macho, possessive types."

Elizabeth was about to reassure him when a sudden banging on the window distracted her attention. Turning, she found herself face to face with Sam.

"Wait there!" Sam shouted through the glass. He practically ran the length of the Dairi Burger and flung himself in the seat next to Todd. "I'm so glad I found you two," he said.

"What's wrong, Sam?" she asked.

He put his helmet on the floor by his feet. "I've been going nuts trying to find your sister."

Elizabeth blinked. "Jessica?"

"That's right," Sam said, lowering his voice. "I was going to follow her after school today, but by the time I got to Sweet Valley High she was already gone."

"Follow her!" Elizabeth didn't bother to hide her shock. "What are you talking about, Sam? You know Jessica went to Lila's for supper tonight."

Sam looked skeptical. "I doubt that, Elizabeth."

"What do you mean?" Elizabeth asked indignantly.

Sam explained to Elizabeth and Todd about the fight he and Jessica had had the day before. By the end of his story, he looked even more exhausted than he had when he began. "I knew she was acting strangely, and I knew she was avoiding me," he said sadly, "but I never expected her to lie to me like that." He stared at his hands for a few seconds. "I'm really worried about her."

After hearing Sam's story, Elizabeth was beginning to worry herself. She couldn't help but wonder if Jessica wasn't sneaking out to see another boy. Not that she was going to suggest that to Sam. "I know Jessica's been a little stranger than usual lately," she said lightly, "but I really don't think you should worry. You know Jessica. She goes through phases all the time."

"That's right," Todd chimed in. "One week she's interpreting dreams, and the next week she wants to be a movie star."

Sam's handsome face creased into a frown. "I hope you're right," he said. "But I have this awful feeling that it isn't so simple this time."

Todd and Elizabeth sat in his car for some time talking about Jessica and Sam.

"I don't know," Todd said. "Normally, I'd agree that Jessica must be interested in some other guy, but this time I'm not so sure." He made a face. "I mean, we all agree: even for Jessica, she's been acting pretty weird recently."

"It does make sense, though," Elizabeth argued. "All this sweetness and goodness, and those funny clothes . . . Whenever Jessica meets a new boy she always throws herself into whatever he's into. Remember when she had a crush on that protester?"

"What do you think this guy does?" asked Todd. "Run a thrift shop?"

Elizabeth smiled. "I think he's a librarian."

"It does make a strange kind of sense," Todd mused. "After all, she's been spending a lot of time in the library."

"He'd have to be a pretty gorgeous librarian," Elizabeth added.

"I don't suppose you could just *ask* her what's going on?" Todd suggested. "You know, one identical twin to another?"

"Not these days," she said without a second's hesitation. "She'd bite my head off. I can't even make a joke about her room anymore without her throwing a fit."

As Elizabeth got ready for bed, she tried to think of some way to start a conversation with Jessica. What she needed was something neutral that Jessica wouldn't take as criticism. Something they could get excited about together. And then Elizabeth remembered Mr. Wakefield's news at dinner about the Good Friends. Elizabeth snapped her fingers. "That's it!" she said out loud. There was nothing Jessica liked better than some good gossip. Especially about something like this. A cult in Sweet Valley! That was just the thing Elizabeth needed to break the ice that had formed between her and her sister.

"A cult?" Jessica snapped after Elizabeth had gone into Jessica's room and brought up the subject. "I've never heard anything so ridiculous." Her eyes were icy with rage. "You can't just go around accusing innocent people of things like that, Elizabeth."

Elizabeth couldn't believe it. Instead of being surprised and fascinated, Jessica had gotten furious! "I'm not accusing anybody of anything," Elizabeth defended herself. "I'm just telling you what Dad said. His firm's investigating these Good Friends because they may be doing something illegal."

"Well, they're not doing anything illegal," Jessica said briskly. "And they certainly aren't a cult."

Elizabeth looked at her sister closely. She was sitting on her bed, reading something. But there were no piles of clothes on the bed, no stacks of magazines, no dirty towels—just Jessica. Elizabeth found the whole effect a little scary. *What happened to the mess and clutter? What was going on?* All of Elizabeth's determination to be tactful and not to sound critical disappeared. "How do you know so much about the Good Friends?" she blurted out.

Jessica turned back to the page she had been reading. "I've just heard a lot about all the good work they do," she said evasively. "You always see them around, raising money for cancer research, the homeless, orphans, things like that." She raised her head, but though she was looking at Elizabeth she wouldn't meet her eyes. "I just can't believe anyone would accuse them of being a cult, that's all."

"But if they do collect money for so many different charities," Elizabeth persisted, "then there is a chance that Dad's right about them."

"What kind of person are you, Elizabeth Wakefield?" Jessica demanded. "How can you be suspicious of people who have dedicated themselves to doing good?"

"All I meant—"

"I don't care what you meant," Jessica said. "I'm going to sleep." She reached over and snapped off the bedside light, leaving them both in the dark.

Back in her own room, Elizabeth stood against the bathroom door for several minutes, thinking about what Sam had said about Jessica avoiding him and lying to him. She thought about what Todd had said about the girl collecting money in the mall. Then she added those two things to her father's suspicions and Jessica's defense of the Good Friends. Elizabeth climbed into bed and turned off her own light. What she had might not add up to something just yet, but she was going to work on it till it did.

Eight

Jessica told her family that she had to leave the house extremely early on Saturday morning because the cheerleaders from a dozen local schools were getting together at Big Mesa to demonstrate their routines. Her arms filled with her uniform and her pompoms, Jessica climbed into the Fiat. As soon as the red car had disappeared around the corner, Elizabeth went to the phone. She hated to do this, but she felt she had no choice.

Elizabeth took a deep breath, and called Lila Fowler.

"Well," Lila said, "to what do I owe this honor?"

"I wanted to ask you about something," Elizabeth said. "Ever since Jessica was grounded she's been acting really strangely. She studies all the time, and her room's immaculate. I was just a little curious, that's all. I thought that maybe all of you had joined some new club or something?"

"Why are you asking me about Jessica?" Lila snapped.

"Because you're Jessica's best friend," Elizabeth answered. "Who knows her better than you?"

"Practically anybody," Lila said.

"What?"

"Look, Liz, to tell you the truth, I hardly see Jessica anymore, unless I happen to bump into her at school. She's much too busy to spend any time with me."

"But she had dinner with you last night," Elizabeth protested.

"She didn't."

"Then where was she?" Elizabeth asked.

Lila laughed. "She wasn't shopping, that's for sure. Have you seen the clothes Jessica's been wearing lately? She looks like she borrowed them from her great-grandmother."

After Lila hung up, Elizabeth stood for a few minutes staring at the phone, feeling foolish. Even after Sam had told her how Jessica had been lying to him, it hadn't occurred to her that Jessica had been lying to everyone else as well. *Don't jump to conclusions*, she scolded herself. *There still might be some perfectly reasonable explanation for all of this. And, anyway, since when has Lila become such a reliable source of information?*

The first thing to do, Elizabeth decided, was to find out if Jessica really had gone to Big Mesa that morning. She went through a mental list of the people she could call to find out. Not Amy Sutton or Caroline Pearce; both of them were notorious gossips. If Jessica was in some kind of trouble, the last thing Elizabeth wanted was to broadcast it all over Sweet Valley. Finally Elizabeth called Sandra Bacon. Sandra was nice, intelligent, and reliable.

Sandra answered the phone. "Hi, Elizabeth," she said brightly. "What's up?"

"Oh, nothing much," Elizabeth replied, trying to sound casual. "I was just wondering if you were going to Big Mesa today?"

"There's nothing happening at Big Mesa that I know about," Sandra said.

"Oh, I must have the date wrong," Elizabeth said quickly. "I thought there was a game today. Sorry for bothering you, Sandra." Elizabeth said goodbye and put the receiver back in its cradle. "Jessica," she said out loud, "what are you up to now?"

Halfway to the Good Friends' house, Jessica pulled the Fiat over to the side of the road and put her cheerleading things in the trunk. She didn't want Adam or any of the others to see them and ask her why she was riding around with pompoms in the car when she was supposed to be devoting herself to good works. Jessica made a face as she slammed the trunk shut. *Especially not Susan*, she said to herself.

Instead of Susan coming to like and accept her as time went on, she had become even more hostile. Every time Jessica looked up, she caught Susan staring at her, and whenever Jessica was alone with Adam, Susan found some excuse for disturbing them. Once or twice, Jessica was sure, Susan had followed her through the house or the yard, trying to get her alone. But Jessica always managed to avoid her.

All night long Jessica had tossed and turned, thinking about what Elizabeth had told her about the Good Friends. She knew, of course, that none of it was true. Elizabeth was wrong, her father was wrong, and all those charities were wrong. Adam was right: they were all so caught up in their own little worlds that they could not possibly understand the Good Friends and what they were about.

Jessica had been with them long enough to know that there was no way that Adam and the Good Friends could be anything but what they claimed. They were selfless and hardworking. They were total people. Adam wasn't just an ordinary man; he was really and truly special.

The memory of that afternoon in the back of the van, when Adam had taken some of the money they had collected to buy food, floated through her mind, but Jessica dismissed it immediately. That had been a misunderstanding on her part. She smiled at how naive she had been. *Of course the Good Friends need to eat and pay rent, just like anybody else!*

Jessica wasn't worried that what her sister had said might be true. What upset her was how these accusations might affect Adam. What if they turned people against him? What if they destroyed all of the good work he had already done?

Jessica turned onto Cedar Street. A horrible thought occurred to her. What if Adam became angry with *her* because of what Mr. Wakefield's firm was doing to him? What if he asked her to stay away from the group? What if he decided to leave town?

By the time Jessica arrived at the house, most of the Good Friends had already left for a day of collecting. Annie, Ted, and Brian were in the kitchen, cleaning up from breakfast.

Annie greeted her with a big hug. "I always miss you when you're not here," she said.

Ted looked up from the pan he was scrubbing. "Me, too. I really feel like you're part of us now."

Annie put her arm through Jessica's. "Adam says so, too," she whispered. "He says your absence is like a boarded-up window in our home."

Normally, Jessica would have been delighted to hear that, but today she had more important things on her mind. "Where is Adam?" she asked, trying to keep the urgency out of her voice. "I have something I want to talk to him about."

"Oh, you can't talk to him now," Annie said. "He's upstairs, working in his room."

Jessica slipped her arm from Annie's. "It won't take a minute," she said, heading toward the stairs.

"Jessica!" Brian called, sounding slightly agitated. "We never bother Adam when he's in his room. It's a rule."

"That's right," Ted said. "Adam hates to be disturbed."

Jessica turned in the doorway. "But I'm not going to disturb him. I need to tell him something."

"Can't it wait, Jessica?" Annie pleaded. "Please? You know I hate any trouble."

"But I'm not causing any trouble," Jessica insisted. She turned toward the stairs. *I'm trying to avoid trouble*, she added to herself.

Jessica stood listening outside Adam's door. From inside, she could hear the faint rustle of papers. She knocked. The rustle continued, but there was no answer. Adam was probably working so hard that he hadn't heard her. She knocked a little harder.

"Go away!" came the gruff, impatient answer. "You know the rules."

The voice was so much rougher than the soft and gentle one she associated with Adam Marvel that Jessica wondered for a second if she was knocking on the wrong door. She looked up and down the hallway. No, it was definitely the door to Adam's room. "Adam?" she called. "It's me, Jessica."

She could hear the sound of a chair being pushed back. "Jessica! Why didn't you say it was you?"

A warm feeling of relief surged through her. Adam had probably been so absorbed that he hadn't realized how annoyed he had sounded. Jessica put her hand on the knob and turned it. The door was locked.

"Just a minute!" Adam called. "I'll be right there."

She heard a drawer being closed with a metallic banging sound. Suddenly the door opened and Adam stepped into the hallway, shutting it behind him. "Jessica," he said with a smile, "I'm so sorry. I thought you were one of the others." He lowered his voice in a conspiratorial way. "You know how it is. If I don't make a few rules, there'll be somebody wanting something from me every minute of the day."

"Oh, of course." Jessica nodded. "I understand completely." She cleared her throat. "I wouldn't have bothered you unless it was something really important."

Adam put a hand on her shoulder. "Sure," he said, "shoot."

She looked at the door he was leaning against. "Well," she said slowly, "it's kind of private."

"That's another of my rules," he explained, understanding her look. "I never let anyone into my room." He grinned good-naturedly. "I can't have everyone trooping through, disturbing my work. You wouldn't want anyone to accuse me of favoritism, would you?"

"Oh, no, of course not," Jessica said quickly. She could imagine how someone like Susan might get jealous.

"But no one can hear us here," he assured her. "Everyone's out of the house except for Annie, Brian, and Ted, and they would never eavesdrop."

As calmly as she could, Jessica told Adam everything that Elizabeth had told her. Even though he was the most patient and gentle man she had ever known, she had expected him to be angry or upset by her father's rumors. But not a flicker of emotion showed on his handsome face. Instead, he listened silently but intently, the green eyes staring placidly into hers.

"This sort of thing has happened to the Good Friends before, Jessica," he said sadly. "Because we're so honest and trusting ourselves, I'm afraid that people sometimes take advantage of us."

"You mean like phony charities?" Jessica asked.

"Exactly," he said softly, his voice sounding tired. "You have no idea how many dishonest, manipulative people there are in this world, Jessica, and I wish you didn't have to find out."

"I knew my father was wrong!" Jessica said.

"Don't say *wrong*." Adam smiled understandingly. "Your father's misguided. Like most people, he believes what he wants to believe. The truth is, though, that as soon as I discover that any of the charities we work for aren't genuine, we sever all connections with them." He nodded toward the door to his room. "As a matter of fact, that's what I've been doing all morning. Checking up on things."

Jessica hesitated. "And what about the charities that claim we don't actually give them any money at all?"

"What about them?" he asked. "You don't believe that, do you, Jessica?" He made a face. "What you have to understand about a lot of these big organizations is that they have people skimming money off for themselves."

"You mean, they pretend that they haven't received money and then just keep it?"

"You are a smart girl," Adam said admiringly. "And you're smart enough to realize something else."

Jessica could see her own reflection in those deep, green eyes. "What's that?"

"That most people don't like anyone or anything that's different. That's why they don't like us. They don't want us living in their towns, so they'll do anything to try and get us to leave."

"Like make up lies about the Good Friends and call it a cult."

"Exactly," Adam said, putting an arm around her.

At one o'clock Todd arrived at the Wakefields' to take Elizabeth for a little private bowling practice.

"I'm sorry, Todd," Elizabeth said as soon as she opened the door, "but there's no way I can go bowling this afternoon."

"What's wrong, Liz? What happened?" He followed her into the house.

Elizabeth paced up and down the living room. "I should have known better," she said, biting her lip. "It's all my fault. I should have followed her this morning." She flung her hands in the air. "Oh, why didn't I pay more attention to what she was doing?"

"Calm down," Todd said, encircling her in his

arms. "Does this have something to do with Jessica?"

Elizabeth nodded. "Who else?" She told him about her conversation with Jessica the night before, including what her father had said about the Good Friends and their activities, and about the calls she had made to Lila and Sandra that morning.

"Wow," Todd said when she had finished. "It does look like something very strange is going on here, doesn't it?"

"I have this hunch that it's all tied up with the Good Friends," Elizabeth said.

"Oh, come on, now," Todd said. "Don't go jumping to any wild conclusions here. Jessica may get a little carried away now and then, but I can't believe she'd join a cult."

Just then the doorbell rang three times in a row.

Elizabeth opened the front door, and Sam practically fell into the hallway. His eyes were bright with excitement and his face was flushed. He was talking so fast that it was difficult to make any sense out of what he was saying.

"Slow down, Sam!" Elizabeth said. "I can't understand what you're saying."

Sam took a deep breath. "I was right!" he shouted. "I knew something weird was going on, and I was right."

"Have you found out something about Jessica?" Elizabeth asked.

"I found out where she goes," he announced triumphantly. "I followed her when she left home this morning." He grabbed hold of Elizabeth's hand. "You've got to come with me!" he pleaded. "Now! This very minute!"

"Of course we'll come," Elizabeth said. She turned to Todd. "Right?"

Todd shrugged. "What, and miss bowling?"

Sam turned the car down Cedar Street. "We're almost there," he told them.

Elizabeth peered through the window. "This can't be right," she said skeptically. "Jessica would never come to a neighborhood like this."

"She came here, all right," Sam said.

"Look!" Todd said, leaning over the front seat. "There's your car!"

Elizabeth gasped. There, in front of one of the most rundown houses on the block, was the red Fiat. "I don't believe this," she mumbled.

"It doesn't look like anybody's home," Todd said. "But to be safe we'd better drive around the corner and come back on foot."

"Who do you think lives here?" Elizabeth whispered as they tiptoed up to the ramshackle old house. A quick reconnaissance by Sam had convinced them that it was empty, but they weren't going to take any chances. There might still be someone upstairs.

"Look at that," Todd said, pointing to the porch. Hanging from the eaves was a small, hand-painted sign: The Good Friends.

"What did I tell you?" Elizabeth cried. "She is involved with that group!"

Sam looked at Elizabeth. "What group?"

"You're jumping to conclusions again," Todd said. "Maybe she's not really involved with the group. Maybe she's just friendly with someone who is."

Sam looked at Todd. "What group?"

"And what about that girl you saw at the mall, Todd? The girl you said reminded you of Jessica? Don't you think she was probably part of this cult?" Elizabeth persisted.

A look of alarm came over Sam's face. "Cult? What do you mean, cult? Will one of you please tell me what's going on?"

Elizabeth quickly told him all she knew about the Good Friends.

"That's it," Sam said as soon as she was done. "I say we wait here for them to come back, and we take Jessica home with us."

Elizabeth shook her head. "No," she decided, "that will make Jessica more determined than ever."

"I think we should go straight to your parents and tell them what we know. Your father's a lawyer—he'll be able to handle this," Todd said.

Elizabeth shook her head again. "No," she said quickly, "that won't work, either. I know Jessica. If we drag our parents into this, she'll think everyone's against her, and then there's no telling what she'll do."

"All right," Todd said, "but we've got to do something."

Sam nodded. "And pretty quick, too."

105

"Let's go home. I'll talk to her there." Elizabeth said firmly. "Alone."

"Better you than me," Sam mumbled.

Jessica had changed a lot in the last couple of weeks, but not so much that it was easy to make her see reason.

"How dare you follow me!" she screamed at Elizabeth. "What gives you the right to treat me like I've committed some sort of crime?"

"Jessica, please," her sister pleaded, "just calm down for a minute. I wasn't following you because I thought you'd done something wrong. I followed you because I was worried about you."

"It's the same thing!" Jessica shouted. "You always treat me like I'm stupid. I can take care of myself, you know!"

"If you can take care of yourself, then why did you lie about where you were going?" Elizabeth asked.

Jessica put her hands on her hips. "Because I didn't think you'd understand. And I was right!"

"No, you weren't right," Elizabeth argued. "You never gave me a chance to understand."

Jessica stared at her twin for several seconds, clearly thinking about what Elizabeth had just said.

"If you'd explained what was happening, I would have tried to see it from your side. You know I would have," Elizabeth said. "Instead, you lied to everyone and started sneaking a—"

"You're right, Elizabeth," Jessica interrupted her. "You're absolutely right. How can I expect you to see how much the Good Friends have done for me, when I've acted like I was doing something wrong?"

Elizabeth was so surprised by her sister's about-face that she gaped at her in silence.

"Do you want to hear about them, Liz?" Jessica asked, suddenly as sweet as sugar. "Are you really interested?"

"Of course I'm interested," Elizabeth said quickly.

Thirty minutes later, Jessica finished her tribute to Adam Marvel and the Good Friends. "So you see," she explained for the fourth time, "these people are good and sincere. They're not shallow and selfish, like the people I used to hang out with." She smiled. "I can't tell you how wonderful it makes me feel to be working with them. For the first time in my life I feel like I'm really being useful."

Elizabeth couldn't argue with the fact that Jessica's old friends, such as Lila and Amy, were pretty self-centered and shallow. Nor could she argue that there was anything wrong with helping others. She sighed. "It sounds like this group has done you a lot of good," she said slowly. "But that doesn't change what Dad was saying."

"But I told you," Jessica insisted. "Adam explained it all to me. The Good Friends are completely honest, but sometimes they get mixed up with the wrong sort of charities by mistake."

"I don't know," Elizabeth said doubtfully.

"I'll tell you what." Jessica looked directly into her sister's eyes. "I'll make you a promise."

"A promise?"

"I promise you that if you don't say anything about this to anybody, I'll drop the Good Friends immediately if it turns out that there is any truth to what Dad was saying."

"Immediately?" Elizabeth repeated.

Jessica crossed her heart. "Absolutely."

"You promise?"

"I promise."

Nine

Elizabeth spent most of Monday and Tuesday worrying about her sister. Driving home from school on Tuesday afternoon, she finally confided in Enid.

Enid listened thoughtfully while Elizabeth talked.

"I just can't seem to concentrate on anything else," Elizabeth concluded. "I think I was right not to tell Mom and Dad, because I don't want to force Jessica into doing something drastic. But at the same time, I'm terrified that if something awful does happen, it'll be all my fault."

Enid gave a low whistle. "Jessica's been in some outrageous situations in the past, but this time she's outdone herself."

"I guess practice really does make perfect," Elizabeth joked halfheartedly. She pulled up in front of Enid's house. "I don't know," she sighed.

"I could imagine Jessica running off to Colorado because of some ski instructor or something, but I never in a million years dreamed she'd get into something like this."

"I know what you mean," Enid agreed. "It seems really weird to be worried about Jessica because she's dedicating herself to doing good."

Elizabeth laughed.

"Still," Enid said reassuringly, "Jessica did promise that if it turns out that this organization isn't legitimate, she'll drop it immediately, right?"

Elizabeth nodded.

"Then what's the problem? You have to trust her, don't you? Or are you afraid she won't keep her word?"

"Oh, of course I think she'll keep her word," Elizabeth answered quickly, not wanting to consider the possibility that she wouldn't. "I just wish I knew what this group was really like. I mean, my father says one thing and Jessica says the opposite. If only I could find out the truth for myself. . . ."

Enid shook her head. "You can't exactly knock on the door and say, 'Hi, I'm Jessica's sister, I want to see for myself if you're running a cult here.' "

An enormous smile suddenly appeared on Elizabeth's face, and her eyes sparkled with excitement. "Enid!" Elizabeth shrieked. "You're a genius!" She honked the Fiat's horn. "At last, I have a plan!"

Elizabeth's plan was brilliant in its simplicity. She and Jessica were so identical that even their parents sometimes had difficulty telling them apart. Why not impersonate Jessica and see the Good Friends for herself firsthand?

After dropping Enid off, Elizabeth worked out the details in her mind as she drove home.

Halfway to Calico Drive, she turned the Fiat around and headed back toward the Wilkinses' home. Foolproof though her scheme was, she was still going to need some help.

"So it's decided," Elizabeth said, pushing her empty plate to one side. She, Todd, and Sam were in the Dairi Burger, discussing the role each of them would play in her little drama. "Sam will keep Jessica busy tomorrow night, while I infiltrate the Good Friends." She pointed to Todd. "And *you* will lurk outside that creepy house, in the unlikely event that I need some help."

Todd look worried. "I don't know. It seems pretty risky."

"I think Elizabeth's right," Sam argued. "It's perfect. There's no way these people are going to be able to tell she isn't Jessica. Admit it, Todd, I bet there are times when even you can't tell who is who."

Todd still looked reluctant. "It just bothers me that we know so little about them," he explained. "I mean, what if they have some crazy nickname for Jessica? These people do that a lot. You know, they might call her Shaheena or Bright Star or something. Elizabeth could easily give herself away."

111

Elizabeth reached over and took his hand. "Todd," she said in her most reasonable voice, "you're letting your imagination run away with you. All I have to do is keep my mouth shut and let them lead the way. Trust me. I've done this before. It'll be all right."

"You've never done it in this sort of situation before," Todd countered. "What if they kidnap you? Have you thought of that?"

Elizabeth kissed his cheek. "That's why you'll be outside, waiting to rescue me if anything goes wrong."

Todd still looked skeptical, but it was obvious that he had been won over. "Oh, sure," he said, "Todd Wilkins and his killer tennis racquet." He gave Elizabeth a rueful smile. "Let's hope you don't need any assistance."

Elizabeth sat on her sister's perfectly made bed, watching Jessica get ready for her date with Sam.

"Don't you think you should wear something a little more colorful?" she asked. "I mean, you're going to a movie, not a funeral."

Jessica shot her a look. "Don't push it, Elizabeth. I'm only going on this date because you blackmailed me."

Elizabeth's eyes widened innocently. "I didn't blackmail you. I only said that I'd done you a favor, keeping quiet about the Good Friends, and the least you could do was put poor Sam out of his misery for one night."

"What about *my* misery?" Jessica retorted.

"Wednesday night is discussion night at the Good Friends. I may be missing something really interesting."

"You used to think Sam was really interesting," Elizabeth reminded her.

"I used to think Ken and Barbie were really interesting, too," she snapped.

As soon as Jessica and Sam drove away, Elizabeth hurried back into her sister's room, rummaged through the closet, and transformed herself into the colorless and old-fashioned version of her twin. *Thank goodness Mom and Dad are having dinner out tonight,* Elizabeth thought as she walked through the kitchen and out to the Fiat. *I'd hate to have to explain to them why I look like this!*

She picked up Todd on the way to the Good Friends' house. "Now remember," he said every few minutes, "if there's any sign of trouble, you just scream."

"Get down," Elizabeth hissed. "We're almost there. The last thing we need is for one of them to spot you."

Todd hunkered down on the floor. "Now remember," he said as she climbed out of the car, "if there's any trouble—"

The door slammed shut. "I'll remember," she whispered. Elizabeth faced the house. *Here I go!* she told herself. She marched purposely up the front path. At the door she hesitated for a second. Should she knock? Or should she walk right in? *Walk in,* she decided. *After all, Jessica practically lives with these people. She spends more time at this rickety old house than she used to spend at the mall.*

113

Elizabeth put on the vague, slightly plastic smile that Jessica had been wearing lately. She pushed open the front door and stepped into the hallway.

The Wednesday-night discussion meeting was already under way. About a dozen people were sitting in the living room, expressions of intense concentration on their faces.

Here goes nothing! Elizabeth told herself. "Hi!" she called brightly, sounding remarkably like her twin. "I'm so glad I could make it tonight after all."

"It's Jess!" one of the boys called out.

The others all turned and smile.

"Come on in and sit down!" one of the boys said. He turned to a nervous-looking girl. "Annie, you and Susan move over."

Elizabeth walked in, feeling as though all eyes were on her. Annie and Susan made room for her on the couch. Annie squeezed her arm. "I'm glad you could make it, too," she whispered. "It's just not the same when you're not here. Even Adam says you always add so much to the discussions."

Elizabeth's heart sank a little, thinking of Todd's fears. She could only hope that Adam wasn't expecting her to contribute much to the discussion tonight. "I wouldn't miss one for the world," she whispered back. And then she looked around her, trying not to seem curious.

That must be Adam Marvel! Elizabeth decided as she looked at the man who was speaking, trying to keep her amazement from showing on her face. *He doesn't look anything like a cult leader*, she thought to herself. *And he certainly isn't old. He's handsome!*

And then she realized that he knew she was staring at him. All at once, she was looking right into those eyes, and they were looking right into hers. He smiled, a slow, thoughtful smile. Elizabeth couldn't help wondering if he somehow knew she wasn't Jessica. *That's ridiculous*, she assured herself. *He can't know*. The smile deepened, and then he opened his mouth to speak. *He does know!* she thought in a panic. *And he's going to speak to me!* All Elizabeth could hear was the pounding of her heart.

Suddenly Adam turned to one of the boys. "Ted," he said, in a voice as sweet as syrup, "what do *you* think are the most important goals a person can have in his life?"

Ted, like the others, had been gazing at Adam as though the sun were shining through Adam's eyes. "Oh, I agree with you completely. Loyalty and selflessness are the most important things a total person can strive for."

"Sky?" Adam asked, smiling at one of the other boys. Elizabeth couldn't help noticing that there was no smile in those green eyes.

"Absolutely," Sky said in a soft, timid voice, "you're absolutely right."

Some discussion, Elizabeth thought.

"Annie?" Again Adam Marvel smiled, and again the ice-green eyes remained hard.

Annie's voice quivered. "Oh, yes," she said breathlessly. "Yes, I completely agree."

Marbles, Elizabeth decided as the green eyes came to rest on her again. *They remind me of clear marbles.*

"What about you, Jessica?" Adam asked.

Was it her imagination, or had he emphasized the word *Jessica?*

"You're our newest member." Adam smiled. "Maybe *you* have some different ideas." His voice was so smooth, it made her spine prickle.

Elizabeth smiled back, willing her voice not to shake. "Oh, no," she said quietly but ardently. "No, I have no different ideas. I think everything you said is totally true."

Adam Marvel leaned back in his chair. "It gives me such a good feeling to be part of such a harmonious group," he said with satisfaction.

There was a murmur of agreement from the rest of the group.

She could still feel Adam Marvel watching her. How was it possible to be afraid of someone who smiled so much? *I don't think I'm going to be able to take much more of this,* Elizabeth said to herself. *I have to get out of here.*

Just then, almost as though her wish had been answered, the front door was flung open and several people, all of them obviously Good Friends, rushed into the room, talking at once.

Adam was on his feet instantly. "What's wrong?" he asked, his voice as smooth and unemotional as ever.

Elizabeth had to concentrate to follow the story. It seemed that a small group of Good Friends had been out collecting money when one of them named Brian had disappeared.

Adam turned to a dark, slender boy named Daryl. "What do you mean, he disappeared?"

"We just lost him somehow," a tall, fair girl, dressed in almost the same style skirt and sweater that Elizabeth had taken from Jessica's closet, whispered nervously.

Elizabeth kept her eyes on Adam. He was still calm and smiling, but she saw that those glass-green eyes were showing some real feeling for the first time that evening. A little chill ran through her. The feeling they were showing was rage.

"People just don't disappear in shopping malls," Adam said evenly. "There must be some logical explanation."

"We looked everywhere, Adam," Daryl said. "We even had him paged. He just vanished into thin air!"

Elizabeth's eyes fell on Adam Marvel's hands. They were hanging by his side, but his fists were clenched so tightly that his knuckles were white.

Adam smiled broadly. "Well, Daryl, you're going to have to find him, aren't you?"

Elizabeth felt chilled by the threat she heard in Adam's words. But when she looked at the others they were still grinning. Their smiles reminded Elizabeth of the smiles painted on dolls.

"In case Brian comes back, Susan, Jessica, and I will stay here," Adam announced. "The rest of you go back to the mall with Daryl." He shook a finger at them. "And don't come back without him." He laughed a laugh that to Elizabeth's ears contained no humor.

Except for Elizabeth and the girl named Susan, all the Good Friends walked out the door and across the lawn to where the van was parked in the drive. Adam went with them. Elizabeth could hear his voice from the darkness outside, organizing the others. She was so intent on hearing what he was saying that it took her a few seconds before she realized Susan was speaking to her in an anxious whisper. "What?" Elizabeth asked.

Susan's dark eyes were filled with fear. "Get out of here and don't come back," Susan hissed. She grabbed Elizabeth's arm and gave it a yank. "Now!" she urged her. "Before it's too late!"

Elizabeth automatically pulled away. "What do you mean?" she whispered back. "Why should I—"

The front door slammed shut. Without looking over, Elizabeth knew that Adam had returned, because she saw Susan flinch.

"What are you two whispering about?" asked the soft, easy voice.

Elizabeth turned, the Good Friends' smile firmly stuck on her face. "I was teasing Susan about wanting to go along because she has a crush on Brian," she said, thinking quickly.

Adam raised one elegant eyebrow. "Now, you know better than that, Jessica. Good Friends don't get crushes." He turned his smile on Susan. "Do they, Susan?"

Elizabeth thought she could see a glimmer of menace in the green eyes. She glanced at Susan.

From the expression on her face, she was sure that Susan had seen it, too.

Sam held the door of the movie theater open for Jessica. "So, what did you think of the film?" he asked as he followed her out.

Jessica shrugged. She had enjoyed the film because it had meant that she didn't have to speak to Sam, but other than that she hadn't really liked it at all. Adam discouraged them from seeing movies. He said that movies, like television, gave people a false idea of what the world was like, and stopped them from thinking. "Who wants to sit in a dark, stuffy room, watching some silly film, when you could be doing some good in the world?" Adam always said.

Sam slipped his arm through hers. "Was that a 'not bad' shrug or an 'I hated it' shrug?"

Jessica knew that he was trying to get her to joke with him, and she wished he would stop. He was getting on her nerves. First he kept asking her about cheerleading and Pi Beta Alpha, two childish, self-indulgent activities she had no interest in anymore. Then he made a comment about liking her better the way she used to be, and seemed hurt when she accused him of not letting her be herself. "If you want to know the truth," she said in a bored voice, "I thought the film was pretty shallow."

"Shallow?" Sam asked. She could tell from his tone that he had thought the movie was great.

Another thing Adam always said was that you

should respect other people's feelings. "If you can't say something nice," Adam always said, "then try not to say anything." Jessica decided that she should be nicer to Sam. After all, it was not really his fault that he wasn't a total person. He had been misled and misguided, just as she had been.

She turned to him with a smile. "But I can see why you liked it," she said pleasantly. "That sort of humor appeals to people who want to escape from reality."

Sam gave her a look. "You think *I'm* trying to escape from reality?"

"Oh, it's all right," Jessica said, still smiling. "I'm not saying there's anything wrong with that. It's just a little immature."

"Gee, thanks," Sam mumbled. "That's very understanding of you."

"I'd rather read a book to help me improve myself than go to a movie," Jessica continued as they walked toward Sam's car.

"And what about now?" Sam asked. "Would you rather have a burger or a pizza?"

Jessica had been looking forward to getting home and reading another chapter in the book Adam had loaned her. Then she had planned to write three positive thoughts in the journal Adam had told her to start. Adam said that keeping a diary encouraged discipline. She glanced at Sam, trying not to look too horrified by the suggestion that they spend even more time together. "I'm not really hungry," she said, flashing him one of her brighter smiles. "Actually," she continued, stifling a yawn, "if you want to know the truth, I'm pretty tired."

"Maybe for once I don't want the truth," Sam said. "Why don't you lie to me and say you'd like to go for a pizza?"

Elizabeth and Todd were sitting in the Wilkinses' kitchen, having a soda and going over the events of the night.

"I really wish you'd tell your parents," Todd said. "I can't tell you how scared I was when I saw all those people running into the house. I was sure they were going to take you away with them in their van."

Elizabeth squeezed his hand affectionately. "I was pretty scared myself," she said. "Especially when that girl, Susan, told me to get out while I could." She shuddered at the memory. "I don't know what's going on there, but I know it isn't good."

"All the more reason to tell your parents," Todd persisted. "Especially if you're right about this Marvel guy trying to persuade Jessica to move in with the group."

"He didn't say that in so many words," she explained, "but he did drop a couple of hints. About how nice it was when Jessica was there, and how the others all looked up to her. . . ." She laughed nervously. "He really gives me the creeps."

"In that case—"

"I know," she said, "talk to my parents. But I

did promise Jessica I wouldn't. And she promised me that if there was any proof about the Good Friends being a cult, she'd drop out. So if I can just make her see things the way I saw them tonight . . ."

Todd leaned his head against Elizabeth's. "This is Jessica Wakefield we're talking about here. How are you going to make her see things through your eyes?"

"I'm a Wakefield, too, you know," Elizabeth said. "Jessica's not the only stubborn woman in the family."

"Oh, I didn't doubt that for a minute," he said.

Ten

All night long, Elizabeth's dreams were haunted by the smiling face of Adam Marvel. He followed her everywhere. He went to school with her; he came home with her; it was he, and not Justin Silver, who stood behind her as she bowled. Elizabeth tried to wake up, to get out of her dream, but Adam Marvel just stared at her with those hard green eyes. "Come with us," he repeated over and over again. "We know how to make you happy."

On Thursday morning, Elizabeth was so relieved to wake up and find herself in her own bed, with no one smiling at her but the sun, that she nearly cried out in joy.

That does it! she decided as she leapt out of bed. *I'm telling Jessica everything, and I'm telling her now!* Full of purpose and determination, Elizabeth threw a robe over her pajamas and marched into her sister's room.

Jessica was sitting in her immaculately clean room, at her perfectly neat desk, writing in a notebook. She was already dressed, in brown slacks and a pale blue blouse. Her golden hair, held back with a dark blue barrette, sparkled in the sunlight. She looked up with a happy smile. "I'll be right down, Elizabeth," she promised. "I just want to finish this little bit of homework for English. It's not due till tomorrow, but I'd like to get it in early."

Elizabeth was struck by how *right* everything seemed. *What's wrong with this picture?* she asked herself. And the logical answer was: *Nothing*. Jessica was happy. Jessica was being serious and responsible, just as everyone had always wanted her to be. It was only in her heart that Elizabeth knew that everything was very wrong.

"Did you want to tell me something, Elizabeth?" Jessica asked.

Elizabeth just stood there, speechless. Up until this minute, everything had seemed clear. The Good Friends were a horrible cult, Adam Marvel was a manipulative creep. Awful things were going on there, and if Jessica didn't get away from them, awful things would happen to her. All Elizabeth had to do was tell Jessica what she had seen. But now, standing in her sister's sunny bedroom, watching her do her homework, Elizabeth suddenly realized that she hadn't *seen* anything. Not anything that would serve as proof. All she had were her feelings. Jessica had sat in that same room, with those same people, and had completely different feelings. What could Elizabeth say to her? That she hadn't liked the way Adam Marvel smiled or the way the Good Friends hung on Adam's every word? Even Susan and her warning seemed less sinister in the morning light. In fact, the warning itself hadn't upset her half as much as the look in Adam Marvel's eyes when he had come back into the room. What proof was that? *Well, Jessica, I think Adam gave Susan this really mean look. No, I don't know if he overheard what she said. No, he didn't threaten her or anything.*

"Well?" Jessica interrupted her thoughts. "Elizabeth, was there something you wanted to talk about?"

Elizabeth shook her head. "No," she said. "It was nothing."

To get her mind off her troubles, Elizabeth went into downtown Sweet Valley with Enid after school to help Enid look for a birthday present for her mother. "What I want is something special, exquisite, thoughtful, luxurious, and glamorous, but cheap," Enid joked as they drove down Main Street.

Elizabeth laughed. "How about some exotic bubble bath? Passion flower, avocado, and kiwi, or something?"

"You're a genius!" Enid exclaimed as Elizabeth pulled the Fiat into a parking space. "A total genius! My mother will love it!"

Elizabeth smiled wistfully. "I wish everything was as easy as that."

Enid, who had just been told all about the previous night's visit to the Good Friends, gave Elizabeth a sympathetic smile. She put her arm through Elizabeth's as they headed up the street. "I'll tell you what," she said. "Let's go to the Bath House and get the bubble bath, and then I'll treat you to a milkshake at the Dairi Burger. I think you're too preoccupied with cults and sinister but handsome criminals. You need a dose of normalcy, and there's nothing more normal than the Dairi Burger!"

"You're on!" Elizabeth said, laughing. "A chocolate milkshake is just what I need to feel like a regular teenager again!"

But a half-hour later, as they were walking back to the car, it was Enid who seemed to have lost her grip on reality. While Elizabeth chattered about bath oils and natural sponges, Enid kept turning nervously around to look behind them.

"What is it?" Elizabeth asked. "Did you leave something in the store?"

Enid shook her head. "It's the weirdest thing. When we were picking out the bubble bath, I had this feeling that somebody was watching us through the window. And now I think someone may be following us."

Elizabeth swung around quickly. There were two women with strollers, and a few kids talking loudly. "I don't see anyone suspicious," she reported. "Are you sure you're not seeing things?"

"I don't know," Enid said. "I was sure I kept catching a glimpse of someone when we were in the Bath House. But every time I turned around for a good look, he was gone." She shook herself.

"I guess maybe your story about last night with the Good Friends had more of an effect on me than I thought."

"I guess so," Elizabeth said, trying to make light of the whole thing. But secretly, she was a little worried herself. *Had Adam Marvel realized that she wasn't Jessica, that he was being tricked?* Even Elizabeth had to smile. *And what?* she asked herself. *He had you followed by one of the Good Friends, and is planning to kidnap you and take you away with him?* Elizabeth shook her head as they crossed the parking lot. *Elizabeth Wakefield,* she scolded, *you're not in a mystery novel, you're in Sweet Valley, California. Things like that don't happen here!* She opened the door of the Fiat. "I think we'd better make it two double-chocolate shakes." She laughed. "I have the feeling we really need them."

They started toward the Dairi Burger. "Did I tell you Steven might be coming home next weekend?" Elizabeth asked, determined to make the conversation as normal as possible.

"That's nice," Enid said. She was staring into the rearview mirror.

"Enid. Did you hear what I said?"

"Um," Enid said, leaning forward to get a better view.

"Okay," Elizabeth teased. "Now what? Don't tell me, we're being followed by a black Ford."

"No," Enid said. "It's a silver Porsche."

Elizabeth glanced into the rearview mirror. "There's no silver Porsche behind us," she said, surprised at how relieved she felt. "It's a red Jeep."

"It dropped back," Enid said. "It's at least three cars behind us now."

Elizabeth turned into the Dairi Burger. "Now I know you're definitely hallucinating," she said as she turned off the engine. "There's no way anybody in the Good Friends drives a silver Porsche. All they have is a beat-up old van. I saw it last night."

"Oh." Enid raised one skeptical eyebrow. "What about this Marvel guy? If he's keeping all the money for himself, he probably has a dozen Porsches hidden away."

"You're hallucinating," Elizabeth repeated firmly, hustling Enid into the restaurant before she could see the silver Porsche just disappearing around the corner. *It's coincidence that it seemed to be following us,* Elizabeth told herself. *And Adam Marvel does not own a Porsche.*

Enid was right about one thing: there was nothing more normal than the Dairi Burger. It was filled with people they knew from school, all of them talking and laughing and looking incredibly average. Even Elizabeth could almost forget the empty smiles of Adam Marvel and the Good Friends in this atmosphere.

She took a long sip through her straw. "I think these double-chocolate milkshakes are working already," she said, smiling at Enid.

Enid didn't smile back. "Blond hair, a little long, silver sunglasses, and the profile of a Greek god," she said flatly.

Adam Marvel! Elizabeth thought immediately. She glanced out the window, but there was no one there. She threw the wrapper from her straw at Enid's head. "What are you talking about?" she demanded.

"The guy in the Porsche," Enid said. "He just drove around the back."

"Well, that doesn't mean anything," Elizabeth reasoned, as much for her own benefit as Enid's. "Maybe he's hungry." She nodded her head, agreeing with herself. "That's it. He just happened to be driving along behind us, and he saw us turn in here and realized he was hungry, too."

"I'm sure it's the same person who was watching us when we were buying my mother's present," Enid persisted.

"Enid," Elizabeth reminded her, "you said you didn't actually see anyone."

"I said that when I turned around there was no one there. But I definitely had an impression of someone standing outside." She leaned forward. "Someone blond and incredibly good-looking."

Two or three tense minutes passed while both girls kept their eyes on the front door. No one who looked even vaguely like Enid's description of the driver of the Porsche went in or out.

"Well?" Elizabeth asked. "Now are you satisfied?"

"I think I'm going to need another drink," Enid said. She turned toward the counter.

"I never realized before what an overactive imagination you have." Elizabeth laughed. "You almost had me believing you!"

Enid made a sound somewhere between a gasp and a squeak. "Elizabeth!" she hissed. "Don't turn around, but it's him. He's coming through

129

the kitchen door, and he's got something behind his back. Get down, Elizabeth, I think it's a gun."

Without a second thought, both Elizabeth and Enid dove under the table.

"It's too late," Enid whispered as a pair of male legs stopped right in front of them. "He saw us!"

Elizabeth closed her eyes and held her breath. *This was it! Everything she had imagined about Adam Marvel and the Good Friends had been true. All of Todd's fears and Enid's imaginings had actually come true!*

"Elizabeth," said a soft, laughing voice that did not belong to either Enid or Adam Marvel. "What are you doing under there?"

Elizabeth opened her eyes only to find herself staring into an enormous bunch of flowers and the smiling face of Justin Silver. "I know you said you weren't interested in me," he said with a grin, "but this is a little extreme."

"Justin!"

"I followed you from town." He held the flowers toward her. "I wanted to give you these. To apologize if I've offended you. And to beg you to come back to bowling. I missed you last night."

Elizabeth couldn't answer. She was laughing too hard.

"Remember what I was telling you about that group, the Good Friends, the other night?" Mr. Wakefield asked at supper that night.

Jessica, who had been hurrying through her meal to get back to the new book Adam had given her, nearly bit her tongue in surprise.

"Of course we remember," Mrs. Wakefield said. "Don't tell me something else had happened."

"Something else has happened," he said grimly. "There's a young man named Brian who was lured into the group about a year ago." He gestured toward the twins. "A boy about Elizabeth and Jessica's age. Anyway, his parents did everything they could to persuade Brian to come back home, but he wouldn't listen to them."

"Oh, those poor people," Alice Wakefield said, a look of pain in her eyes.

Jessica could feel her twin trying to catch her eye, but she kept her gaze on her plate.

"The parents were sure the group was up to no good, and that Brian was being brainwashed."

"Brainwashed?" Elizabeth said.

Jessica became intent upon spearing one pea onto the end of her fork.

"That's right," Mr. Wakefield said. "His personality had undergone a complete change, and they couldn't get him to discuss anything reasonably. To every objection or question they raised, he'd just repeat over and over, 'Adam says,' or 'Adam told us,' or 'That's exactly what Adam said you would say.' "

"This sounds very serious," Mrs. Wakefield said.

"It is," her husband concurred. He put down his fork. "But it has a happy ending. I've been corresponding with his parents for some time, and just before I left the office I had a call from them to tell me they had snatched Brian back!"

Jessica's head snapped up and Elizabeth gasped. "What?" Jessica hissed.

Mr. Wakefield was smiling broadly. "That's right. And as soon as he's had time to recover, they'll bring him back to Sweet Valley to testify against this Adam Marvel character." Mr. Wakefield dropped his napkin onto his empty plate. "With what we've managed to get on this guy, and what we think Brian will be able to tell us, we'll be able to put Mr. Marvel away for quite some time."

Jessica felt as though her head were going to explode. *What was going on?* Her father seemed so certain of what he was saying . . . *But he has to be wrong!* Jessica told herself. *He's wrong! He has to be!*

She pushed her plate away. "If you'll excuse me," she mumbled, "I have an awful headache. I think I'll go to my room."

She was out of the kitchen before anyone could respond. But even as she raced up the stairs, she could hear Elizabeth hurrying behind her.

"Now do you believe what I was trying to tell you?" Elizabeth asked, following Jessica into her room. "How much more proof do you need?"

"That's not proof," Jessica snapped. "It's just opinion."

"OK," Elizabeth said. "Then how about this?"

Jessica listened in stunned silence while Elizabeth told her how she had impersonated her and gone to the Good Friends herself the night before.

"I thought you believed me!" Jessica broke in. "I thought you were on *my* side!"

"I am on your side," Elizabeth said. "I didn't

go there because I didn't believe you. I went there because I wanted to believe you."

She went on to explain how she had felt, sitting in the living room with the group, listening to Adam run everything. "It's as if no one has a mind of her own. It gave me the creeps."

"That proves you don't understand," Jessica countered. "Adam always encourages us to think for ourselves!"

"How can you say that?" Elizabeth asked. "No one has any opinion that isn't Adam's. No one dares to go against him, or displease him, or say anything that might be taken as criticism—" Jessica started to interrupt, but Elizabeth kept talking. Elizabeth told her about what had happened when the group came back without Brian, and about Susan's terrified warning.

"Susan?" Jessica shrieked indignantly, filled with relief. "You think Susan's warning means anything?" She couldn't believe how gullible Elizabeth could be! "Susan's been jealous of me since I first went to the Good Friends. She only said that because she wanted to frighten me."

"What about the look on Adam's face when he came back into the house?" Elizabeth persisted. "I'm telling you, Jessica, he looked really mad."

Jessica snorted. "Adam doesn't *get* mad. He's beyond such petty emotions."

Elizabeth grabbed her sister's hands. "Jessica," she pleaded. "This is serious. I'm getting really scared for you. If you don't promise me that you won't go back to the Good Friends, I'm going to have to tell Mom and Dad."

Jessica could tell that Elizabeth really was frightened, but she knew that was because she didn't understand. She wasn't a total person, so she believed these lies about the Friends. Adam had told her this would happen! Everything that Adam said about the way people reacted had turned out to be completely true.

But Jessica knew that there was no use in trying to explain this to Elizabeth. If Jessica didn't give her twin the assurance she wanted, she would go to their parents.

A smile of conciliation spread across Jessica's face. "OK," she said, sounding resigned, "I'll tell you what. I'll stay away from the Good Friends until it's finally proven that they haven't done anything wrong."

"You mean until it's proven whether or not they've done anything wrong," Elizabeth corrected her.

"Whatever," Jessica said. "Is it a deal?"

Elizabeth nodded, obviously relieved. "Yes," she said, "it's a deal."

Adam said that though a person should always try to be honest, it wasn't always necessary to tell the truth to people who were trying to harm you. Jessica thought about this as she drove the Fiat toward Cedar Street. Although she knew Elizabeth meant well, Jessica also knew that staying away from the Good Friends would really do her harm. That was why she had lied to Elizabeth about never going to the group again. That was why she had lied to her parents about having another date with Sam tonight. She pulled to a stop in the driveway. If she couldn't talk to Adam, she would go insane. Surely preventing that was worth one or two little lies!

Adam listened to Jessica's story with his usual calm, patience, wisdom, and understanding. When at last she finished, he put his arms around her and gave her a hug. "You've been through so much!" he whispered soothingly. "You poor thing."

Jessica sat back on the couch. Adam, seeing how upset she was, had sent the other Friends to their rooms. "Is it true about Brian?" she asked.

"You mean have his parents really kidnapped him? Yes, it's true. They took him from us against his will." A serious, troubled expression came over his face. "You knew Brian. You knew how much he loved us, how much he loved it here. Can you imagine how this could destroy him?"

"What kind of people would kidnap their own son?" Jessica wondered.

"Exactly," Adam said. "You're exactly right, as usual." A look of hope came into his eyes. "Jessica," he said in an urgent whisper. "Jessica, you have to help us get Brian back. His parents were the reason he left home in the first place. They made him unhappy. If we really are his good friends, we can't possibly let him stay their prisoner, can we?"

Jessica frowned. "Of course not. But I don't see what I can do. I mean, I don't know Brian's parents."

Adam leaned toward her, gazing intently into

135

her eyes. "That's just our problem," he said softly. "None of us knows Brian's parents. Not what they look like. Not where they live . . ."

A look of pure joy flashed across Jessica's face. "I've got it! I can find out where Brian's parents live! My father must have the address somewhere in his desk at home. Once we get that, we can talk to his parents and make them see how wrong they are. I'm sure that once they get to know us a little, they'll realize what an awful mistake they've made."

"That's brilliant, Jessica," Adam said. "That's absolutely brilliant." He gave her another hug. "I don't know what I'd do without you, Jessica. I really don't. Especially now."

Jessica detected a new sorrow in his tone. "Especially now?"

"That's right," Adam said. "Susan's mother is ill and she's had to leave us, too. There's no telling when she'll be back. Or even if she'll be back."

Jessica felt that the loss of Susan wasn't a big one, but she remembered that the Good Friends were friends to everyone, and never petty or mean. And besides, she could afford to be generous. Now that Susan was gone, Adam really would need her. "Well, then, we really do have to get Brian back," Jessica said. "And we will, too, if I have anything to do with it!"

Wouldn't you know it? Jessica moaned silently, lying wide awake in the dark. *On every other night*

Mom and Dad are in bed before the late news. Tonight, of all nights, they decide to stay up till dawn! She peered at her alarm clock. It was ten to twelve. Not quite dawn, maybe, but late enough considering that she had been waiting for nearly two hours for her parents to go to bed.

At last she heard her parents' bedroom door shut. *Ten more minutes,* she thought. That would give them plenty of time to get into bed. She put the clock on her stomach and watched the hands move slowly to ten after twelve.

Jessica held her breath as she tiptoed down the stairs, lighting her way with the flashlight the twins usually kept in the Fiat's glove compartment. At the bottom of the stairs she stopped for a few seconds, listening for any sounds. All she could hear was the ticking of the living room clock. She stealthily made her way to her father's study and shut the door behind her. She darted the beam around the room, from the bookshelves to the reading chair to the large mahogany desk. That was where the address would be: somewhere on that desk. The small circle of light bounced over the pen stand and the lamp, the calendar and the Rolodex. *The Rolodex!* Jessica almost shouted out loud. Of course her father would have put Brian's parents' address in there. She quickly flicked through the Rolodex. There it was: *Carotin.* Jessica copied down the address.

Maybe I should be a detective, she said to herself as she sneaked back to bed.

Eleven

Elizabeth came downstairs on Saturday morning looking especially pretty. She was wearing an aquamarine blouse that made her hair shine like gold and her blue eyes sparkle.

"Don't you look nice," Mrs. Wakefield said as Elizabeth entered the kitchen. "Are you going somewhere special with Todd?"

Elizabeth flushed. "Oh, no," she said quickly. "This was the first thing I found to put on." The truth was that she wasn't going anywhere with Todd this morning. She was meeting Justin. Not as a date, of course. Only as friends. He had pleaded so hard and so eloquently to her for a little time together alone that she had finally relented. After the way she had behaved in the Dairi Burger, she felt it was the least she could do. "I'm meeting someone at the mall for brunch," she explained.

"Is there anything you want me to do on my way home?"

Mrs. Wakefield shook her head. "Jessica's already gone into town for me," she said. "She certainly has been acting differently lately. I never thought I'd see the Saturday when Jessica would not only be up before you, but also volunteer to spend the morning doing family errands."

Elizabeth sipped her juice thoughtfully. She had never thought she would see this Saturday, either. *Maybe she's trying to show me that she really does means to stay away from the Good Friends*, Elizabeth told herself. A feeling of relief went through her. Maybe now she could stop worrying about Jessica for an hour or two.

Elizabeth and Justin sat at a small corner table of the café near the artificial waterfall. It was a pleasant setting and the food was delicious, but Elizabeth was feeling both restless and bored.

Justin seemed nervous, and although he had a lot to talk about, it was about himself. If he wasn't telling her how athletic he was, he was telling her how good he was at everything. *He's trying to impress me*, she thought.

"I guess I just have a natural talent for that sort of thing," Justin said, finally ending a long story about a camping trip he had taken to Yellowstone Park. He smiled. "I seem to be doing all the talking, Elizabeth. What about you?"

Elizabeth hid a yawn behind her coffee cup.

"Well," she began, "I can't say that I've ever started a fire by rubbing two sticks together, but—"

"I want to hear all about you," Justin interrupted. "Have you always been so beautiful?"

And that was another thing. He kept complimenting her so outrageously that he never gave her a chance to show him that there was a lot more to her than just a pretty face.

Elizabeth pushed back her plate. She knew, of course, what the problem was. Though Justin had promised that they would be getting together only as friends, he really saw this as a date. He wanted to make her see just how terrific he was while he had the chance. The trouble was that the harder he tried, the more bored she became. If only he would relax and act like a friend instead of a potential boyfriend!

"Why don't we take a walk through the mall?" she finally suggested in desperation. Maybe if they moved around they could find something else to talk about besides his many abilities and her good looks.

"Sure," Justin said. "Whatever you want."

They were strolling along the second level, talking about famous people Justin had almost met, when Elizabeth came to a sudden stop.

Justin stopped, too. "What is it?" he asked, turning to see the stunned expression on her face. "Elizabeth, what's wrong?"

There, standing by a small fishpond, was a girl in a gray skirt and plain white blouse collecting money in a bright green container. Elizabeth recognized her immediately as Annie from the Good

Friends. While Elizabeth watched, one of the mall security guards walked up to Annie and asked her something. The vague, dazed smile on Annie's face changed to a look of indignant outrage. "No, I don't have any I.D.," Annie cried in a loud, clear voice. "I don't have to. I'm a Good Friend!"

"Quick!" Elizabeth whispered, terrified that Annie would see her and think she was Jessica. "Let's go downstairs." She swung around and hurried toward the escalator with Justin right behind her.

Elizabeth's heart was racing. It wasn't just that she hadn't wanted Annie to see her. It was also because Annie had reminded her so much of her twin. The furious and defensive look that had come over her face when the guard came up to her was the same one that Jessica got whenever Elizabeth said anything critical of Adam Marvel or his group.

She didn't stop until they reached the ground level.

"Elizabeth," Justin said again. "Please tell me what's wrong."

She looked into his eyes. They were filled with genuine concern. But concern wasn't enough, Elizabeth realized. To communicate how she felt to Justin would take hours of explaining, and even then he might not understand. *Oh, Todd*, Elizabeth cried to herself. *I wish you were here!*

At about the time that Jessica was supposed to be picking up Mr. Wakefield's dry cleaning, she was sitting in the Fiat with Adam Marvel. He had been waiting on the porch when she pulled up that morning, and had come hurrying down the path to her. For the first time since she had been coming to the group, he hadn't bothered with his usual effusive greetings. "Do you have the address?" he had asked sharply.

He was obviously more concerned about the damage that might be done to the Good Friends than he could let on, Jessica had decided, or he wouldn't have spoken to her so abruptly. "It's in my bag," she had answered quickly.

"Good girl," Adam had praised her. "Let's go for a ride so we can talk in private."

"There's no time to lose," Adam was saying as she parked on a quiet side street. "We've got to get to Brian before his parents brainwash him and bring him back to Sweet Valley to testify against us." He slipped the address into his shirt pocket. "We'd better do it tonight," he decided. "Tomorrow may be too late."

"Adam," she said slowly. "Won't they know that you've brought Brian back to the Good Friends? Won't they just come and take him back?"

Adam ran his fingers through his hair. "That's why we'll all have to leave Sweet Valley," he said regretfully. "We have no choice."

Jessica turned to him in surprise. "Leave Sweet Valley?" she repeated in a whisper. "You mean, go somewhere else?"

Adam nodded. "We can start again someplace new," he told her, staring deeply into her eyes. "All of us." He took her hand. "Think of it, Jessica: a new life, with nothing from the past to stop you from being everything you want to be."

Jessica stared through the windshield. *A new life*, she thought, *a new life where no one expects me to be anything that I don't want to be. Where I don't have to do anything I don't want to do. Where people really need me and depend on me.*

"I'm not sure we can make it without you," Adam pleaded. "I can't tell you what it means to me to be able to count on you. Now that Susan's gone . . . well, I don't know what I'd do without you. Please say you'll come with us."

Jessica thought about the reactions her leaving Sweet Valley would cause. Her parents would be outraged, of course. They wouldn't think she was old enough to take care of herself. They would want to protect her, as though she were a child. Elizabeth would be furious. She would think that this was just another of Jessica's passing interests. *You're going to regret this, just like you always do*, Elizabeth would say. Sam would be upset for a while that there wasn't anyone to watch his dirt bike races, but then he'd find some other girl who enjoyed standing in the mud, and he wouldn't even notice she was gone. And as for Jessica's so-called friends, they would just laugh. Instead of supporting and encouraging her, they would make jokes. She frowned. She could just picture Lila, rolling her eyes. *Can you imagine Jessica going off like that? She'll be back as soon as she runs out of shampoo*, Lila would say. Jessica raised her chin. "I'll be there," she said. "You know you can count on me."

"I'm really sorry, Sam," Jessica said in a weak voice. "I really, really am, but I don't think I'm going to be able to make our date tonight. I feel *so* sick. I think I must have the flu." She coughed loudly. "Every bone in my body aches, and I've got this splitting headache. . . ."

Sam was all sympathy and concern. "Do you want me to come over and keep you company?" he asked. "I don't like to think of you all by yourself, feeling miserable. We could play a game or something."

"Oh, no," Jessica protested quickly. "I'd hate myself if you caught this from me. And anyway, all I want to do is sleep."

"Maybe I could come by for just a little while," Sam said.

"No, really," Jessica groaned. "My mother says there's nothing you can do for this except drink a lot of juice and rest. If I'm feeling better, you could come over tomorrow."

"All right, if you're sure," Sam reluctantly agreed. "I'll call you in the morning."

As soon as she hung up, Jessica jumped out of bed and began throwing things into a canvas bag. She knew she couldn't take much with her, not without making her family suspicious. If they saw her leaving the house with six pieces of luggage and her tape collection, they would be sure to know that something was up. But she should be able to sneak a few of her more precious possessions out of the house.

144

Her eyes went around the room, surveying her belongings. She wouldn't need any of her brightly colored clothes or most of her shoes. Nor would she need her schoolbooks, which was a cheering thought. But Jessica couldn't help a sigh of regret when she realized that she would not need her bikinis or her party dresses, either. It seemed pretty certain that people who dedicated their lives to doing good didn't attend a lot of parties.

Jessica put her favorite sweater, her scrapbook of mementos, and her jewelry box into the satchel, along with a pile of skirts and blouses. She put her cosmetic bag and her hairbrush on top. She picked up her blow dryer and stood holding it for a few moments. Then she put it down. Adam would probably say that total people could exist without a blow dryer.

Jessica summoned up a sense of excitement as she snapped the bag closed. She was off on an adventure! A real adventure. She was no longer a little girl, she was an adult. She looked around the room at all her familiar things. "Goodbye, dresser," she whispered. "Goodbye, bed and bookcase and closet." She picked up the framed photo of her and Elizabeth, taken in the driveway one summer morning when they were washing the Fiat. Their arms were around each other and they were laughing.

All of a sudden, her mood went from excitement to sadness. *She was leaving all this forever!* She would never again sit at her desk talking on the phone when she should be doing her homework. She would never again sit on Elizabeth's bed late at night, talking. Jessica stuffed the photograph into the outside pocket of her bag, snuffling back a tear. *Don't be ridiculous!* she told herself. *You didn't know anything then. You're getting exactly what you want now.* She picked up her things and quickly left the room.

By the evening, Elizabeth had recovered from her panic in the mall. She had been unfair to Justin, expecting him to be like Todd. And she had been unfair to Jessica, feeling uneasy about her just because of an expression on Annie's face. *You have to get back to normal,* she advised herself as she was getting ready to go bowling with Todd. She was just putting on her sweater when the telephone rang. It was Sam.

Elizabeth thought it was a little odd that Sam should be calling, when Jessica had left several minutes ago to meet him. "What's up, Sam?" she asked.

"Listen, I know Jessica told me not to come over, but I was thinking I might drop by anyway if she's still awake."

"Still awake?" Elizabeth asked. "But Jessica left the house at least fifteen minutes ago, Sam."

"Jessica left the house? Where did she go?" Sam asked.

Something that felt like a large icicle suddenly seemed to have lodged itself in Elizabeth's stomach. "Sam, she went to your house. She has a date with you."

"But she doesn't have a date with me," Sam

said. Elizabeth could tell from his voice that an icicle had lodged itself in his stomach as well. "She canceled it because she has the flu."

Elizabeth knew instantly what had happened. Jessica hadn't given up the Good Friends at all! She was lying, just as she had been lying to everyone all along. Why had Elizabeth trusted her?

Elizabeth thought back to how Jessica had looked when she was leaving. Elizabeth had been in the kitchen, and Jessica had called out, "Good-bye!" Elizabeth had glanced through the hallway to where she stood. Elizabeth concentrated. And then she saw it: off to the side by the staircase had been Jessica's purple canvas duffel bag. How blind could she be? While Jessica had kept promising to stay away from the Good Friends, she had really been planning to join them—maybe for good!

"Sam!" Elizabeth shouted, real urgency in her voice. "We've got to go get Jessica. I'm sure she's gone back to the Good Friends, and I don't think we have a minute to lose."

"I'm on my way," said Sam. "I'll pick you up in ten minutes."

Sam had barely hung up when Elizabeth dialed Todd's number.

"I was just about to leave," Todd said.

"Don't come here," Elizabeth ordered. "I have this awful hunch that Jessica's running away with the Good Friends tonight. Meet me and Sam there. And, Todd," added Elizabeth, almost as an afterthought, "I think you'd better get the police."

*   *   *

Jessica was taken aback when she arrived at the Good Friends' house that night. The place had been stripped bare. The brightly colored bedspreads were gone from the windows, the posters and pictures were gone from the walls. Now the house was as cold and rundown on the inside as it was on the outside. Jessica shuddered. It reminded her of the day of her first visit, when she had almost turned right around and gone back home. She remembered seeing the house and thinking how warm and happy her own house was.

Adam, Ted, and Annie were sitting in the living room together, all ready to leave.

"Where is everybody?" asked Jessica, unable to hide her surprise. "I thought we were all going."

Adam got to his feet. "We are," he said, "but the others have gone on ahead in rented cars. We have just enough room in the van for the four of us and all our things." He grinned. "Well?" he asked. "Are we all set?"

Annie and Ted nodded. "We're ready anytime you are," Ted said.

"Jessica?" Adam asked.

Jessica glanced around the cheerless room, thinking of her sunny room on Calico Drive. Then her eyes rested first on Ted and then on Annie. She had never noticed before how they both looked as though they were walking in their sleep. She thought of Elizabeth, her blue eyes shining and a mischievous smile on her face. She had a sudden urge to say that she had changed her mind.

148

"Jessica?" Adam repeated, his voice harder and more insistent. "Jessica, are you ready?"

She looked into his eyes. She couldn't change her mind, not now. She had come too far. "Oh, yes," she said quickly. "My bag's in the car. I guess I'll just follow you."

Adam's laughter echoed coldly through the empty house. "But you can't bring the Fiat," he informed her. "They'd be able to trace it immediately. We'd never get away."

His words seemed to get stuck in her head. *They'd be able to trace it immediately. We'd never get away.* It suddenly occurred to her that "they" had to be the police. Which meant that she wasn't embarking on an adventure; she was escaping like a criminal. She looked again at the drab, stained walls, and at Annie and Ted, smiling at her in a vague, fixed way. Suddenly her mind went back to that day in the van when she had argued with Adam about using the charity money for lunch.

Adam's hand gripped her elbow. "Come on, Jessica," he growled. "Everyone's waiting for us."

She met his eyes again and he smiled.

"Everyone's waiting for *you*, I should say. You're the one who's rescued us," he said, leading her to the front door.

Feeling a little like she was sleepwalking herself, Jessica let herself be led outside. She was dimly aware that Ted and Annie had gotten into the van. She stood beside Adam while he pulled her bag out of the car and threw the keys to the Fiat under the front seat. Then, his arm around her, they started toward the van.

149

At first, Jessica didn't realize what was happening. Adam had just thrown her bag up to Ted when headlights swept across them and a car came to a halt at the end of the driveway.

She heard Adam mumble something under his breath, and when she looked again, Elizabeth was running toward them. Her heart gave a sudden leap.

"Jessica!" Elizabeth shouted. "Jessica! You've got to listen to me. You can't go with these people! You just can't!"

Jessica looked at her in alarm.

"Jessica," Elizabeth begged. "All I'm asking is that you talk to me. That's all, just talk."

Adam's grip tightened on Jessica's elbow and he shoved her toward the open door of the van. "Get in," he ordered. "We don't have time to stand around here arguing."

Elizabeth glared at him. "Why not?" she demanded. "Do you have something to hide? Are you afraid Jessica will realize the truth about you if you don't get her away as fast as you can?"

Adam gave Jessica another push toward the van. "Don't listen to her," he hissed. "She's one of them."

"I am *not* one of them!" Elizabeth shrieked. "I'm your sister! Your twin sister! Jessica, please!" She reached for Jessica's hand, but Adam Marvel blocked her way. "Can't you see what this man's really like?" Elizabeth argued. "He's encouraged you to lie to your friends and your family. He wants to take you away from everyone who really cares about you. Can't you see that he's using you?"

Jessica felt like she was being torn in two. One part of her was shouting, *She's right! Elizabeth's telling the truth!* But the other half was shouting, *She just wants to make you feel stupid. She's one of them. She's lying.*

Jessica put her hands to her ears. "No, he isn't!" she shouted back. "He cares about me. He values me as a person!"

"If he really valued you, he wouldn't make you sneak away with him in the night," Elizabeth argued.

Jessica looked from Adam to Elizabeth. She had never felt so confused before in her life. A hundred different things were running through her mind at once. She wanted to throw herself into her sister's arms, but Adam's gaze held her back. "Adam and the Good Friends need me!" Jessica screamed. "I'm important to them!"

Tears were trickling down Elizabeth's face. "But you're important to us!" she whispered hoarsely. "*We* need you. I need you!"

Jessica felt tears in her own eyes. She opened her mouth to speak, but just then she heard a shout from the porch behind them.

Everyone turned at once. Sam was coming toward them, a lifeless form in his arms. "How do you explain this, Mr. Marvel?" Sam yelled.

"It's Susan!" Jessica gasped.

"Oh, no!" Annie cried from the door of the van. "She's dead! Susan's dead!" Annie started sobbing uncontrollably.

"Sam . . ." Elizabeth said in a tiny voice.

"She's not dead," Sam said, coming up to

151

where they stood. "But she might have been if I hadn't found her." He turned accusing eyes on Adam. "She was upstairs, tied up and gagged, and unconscious."

Jessica was waiting for Adam to offer some reasonable explanation, as he always did, but instead he tried again to hurry her into the car.

"Adam, you said that Susan had gone home," Jessica said, trying to pull back from him.

He held on tight. "I'll explain that later," he muttered, managing at last to get her to the door of the van.

"You'd better explain it now!" Elizabeth said. She pointed behind her to where Todd and the police had just come to a stop at the end of the drive.

"So you see," Susan said, looking around at her audience in the Wakefields' living room, "I'd known Adam didn't trust me, but after he heard me warning Jess—" She smiled. "I mean, Elizabeth, he must have searched through my things and discovered that I was really a reporter and that I'd infiltrated the group to expose him for the fraud he was."

Jessica and Sam sat with Susan on one couch, Steven Wakefield and Cara sat holding hands on the opposite couch, and Todd and Elizabeth sat on the floor. Susan had completely recovered from the incident at the Good Friends, Adam Marvel was in jail, and Susan was explaining to them how all the pieces fit together.

152

Jessica shook her head. "I thought you hated me, and all the time you were trying to warn me."

"You just didn't seem to be the usual type of girl that was drawn to Adam," Susan explained. "I knew it was only a matter of time before you realized yourself what a creep he was. But I was really afraid that it would be too late by then. Once Adam had someone in his power, he didn't like to let them go."

"I can't believe I almost left everything I love for a con artist and a criminal," Jessica said with a shudder.

"Adam has an uncanny ability to lie and lie, yet completely capture people's trust and love," Susan said. "He has been doing that to teenagers all over the country for years. Jessica wasn't a typical victim because she wasn't as vulnerable as most of the people Adam finds. He had to work twice as hard to capture her trust."

Jessica nodded. "Well, I was feeling pretty unloved, then," Jessica said.

"I guess I'm partly to blame for that," Sam said seriously. "I should have seen how depressed and lonely you felt being grounded."

"Well, you certainly came through for me at the end." Jessica smiled. "I'm really sorry about lying to you."

A few minutes later, Elizabeth got up to get some drinks and brownies for everyone from the kitchen, and Todd followed her.

"I owe you an apology, too," Todd said to Elizabeth. "This whole thing with Justin Silver was partially my fault."

"Why do you say that?" Elizabeth asked. The first thing Elizabeth had done when things began to return to normal was confess to Todd all about Justin's interest in her. She had explained that she had been so flattered, she'd let herself get carried away. It wasn't until all the trouble had begun with Jessica that she had realized how much she cared about and depended on Todd.

"Maybe I'd been taking you for granted," Todd said. He smiled. "After all, if anybody's going to flatter your vanity, it should be me."

Steven walked into the kitchen at that moment. "Wow, you two look happy," he said. "All these happy couples . . ." He shook his head.

"What's the matter, Steven?" Elizabeth said. "Aren't you part of a happy couple?"

Steven looked up, and Elizabeth thought she saw an expression of worry in his eyes. "Sure," he said. "Cara and I have never been happier. The only thing is, she's going to London next week."

"But Steven," Elizabeth protested, "she'll only be gone for a week."

"Oh, I know," Steven said with a shrug. "I don't know why, but I'm dreading it."

Find out what's in store for Cara and Steven in Sweet Valley High #83, STEVEN'S BRIDE.

154